CAUGHT BETWEEN COLD STEEL AND HOT LEAD

A low hiss of triumph broke from Murphy as he saw Dusty dashing toward him. Dropping his right hand, the killer slid the thin-bladed Arkansas toothpick from his boot sheath.

It took even a good rifle shot around four seconds to make an aimed discharge at a running target. Dusty counted the seconds as he ran toward Murphy's rock. Then he remembered the knife Murphy carried. There would be no time to find fresh cover. So Dusty made a jumping slide, going rump down along the ground. Up rose Murphy's arm, the knife held Indian-fashion for a downward stab. Before he could send the knife on its way, he saw Dusty's body twist. Dusty smashed the bottom of his foot into Murphy's face, and the kick packed enough force to slam Murphy backward. Before the man could stop himself, he reeled from behind the rock. Up the slope the bushwhacker changed his aim. Caught in the body by a .50-caliber Sharp's bullet, Murphy slammed over, screamed, and lay kicking in agony.

"Get one of them?" demanded one outlaw.

"Murphy," the other replied. "He rolled like a gut-shot rabbit."

Don't Miss These Exciting Dell Westerns by
J. T. Edson

JUSTICE OF COMPANY 2
THE HIDE AND TALLOW MEN
THE FASTEST GUN IN TEXAS
TROUBLED RANGE
SLIP GUN
THE BAD BUNCH
NO FINGER ON THE TRIGGER
THE NIGHTHAWK

McGraw's Inheritance

J. T. EDSON

A DELL BOOK

Published by
Dell Publishing
a division of
Bantam Doubleday Dell Publishing Group, Inc.
666 Fifth Avenue
New York, New York 10103

ISBN: 0-440-20869-6

Reprinted by arrangement with the author

Printed in the United States of America

April 1991

10 9 8 7 6 5 4 3 2 1

OPM

For Rosica Colin,
With Thanks

CONTENTS

McGraw's
Inheritance

Part One
The Hired Gun

1

The men forming the majority of the Bull's Head saloon's customers had been gathering in San Antonio for the past three days. During the Civil War they won fame as the elite of the Texas Light Cavalry, its hard-riding, hard-fighting Company C, and now they congregated at the city of the Alamo to see a friend embark on matrimony. At noon the following day Sandy McGraw's bachelor days ended officially, and his companions from the days when he rode as company guidon carrier aimed to give him a final night to whoop and howl.

At the bar the bridegroom-to-be, a tall, well-built young man with red hair, a good-looking face, wearing range clothes and belting a brace of 1860 Army Colts in open-topped holsters, stood by his onetime sergeant major for a moment.

"Damned if I thought you'd be fool enough to do it, Sandy," stated the tall, gangling, miserable-faced Billy Jack.

"Which same makes the two of us," Sandy admitted frankly. "Hell, a man has to put down roots some time and Uncle Seth leaving me that spread up San Garcia way's give me a chance of doing it."

"San Garcia country, huh?"

"Sure. Know it?"

"Been up that ways once. It's not bad country. Got gila monsters up there the size of Mississippi alligators and horned toads as big as jackrabbits. You won't need to buy ropes neither. Just catch a rattler and splice a honda into its tail; they come long enough for that. Say, you like hunting, don't you?"

"Yep," said the interested Sandy.

"Get plenty up there. Wolves, cougar, black b'ar, grizzly," Billy Jack explained dismally. "Course, they've done ate off all the elk, deer, and pronghorns, but they grow plenty fat on your cattle."

Listening to the doleful discourse, Sandy felt better. Unless his old sergeant major had changed since the war—as hardly seemed likely—the San Garcia country ought to make a mighty good home for a young feller aiming to settle down and raise him a family.

"Allus did like fat varmints." Sandy grinned and nodded in the direction of a group of laughing, talking men. "Being married's not done ole Red any harm."

"Plumb ruined him is all," replied Billy Jack. "Why, he don't get into no more'n two fights a week since he's been hitched."

The man in question did not look too bad an advertisement for the hardships and horrors of married life. Six feet in height, with a fiery thatch of unruly hair topping a freckled, pugnaciously handsome face, Red Blaze had wide shoulders and a powerful young frame. Nor did entering the state of matrimony appear to be detrimental to his choice of clothing. A low-crowned, wide-brimmed Texas-style Stetson hat hung back on his shoulders, suspended by its storm strap. Around his throat a tight-rolled and knotted bandanna trailed long ends over the front of his blue shirt, presenting a gorgeous riot of color equaled in the room only by that about Sandy's neck. Made of calfskin, his vest had been specially selected from an animal with a bright deer-red and white hide and was much admired by the assembled company. Maybe Red's Levi's pants looked better pressed and his Justin boots bore a better shine than in his bachelor days, but a man could be excused such affectation when paying a visit to a major city like San Antonio. Around his waist hung a well-made gun belt, walnut-handled Army Colts riding butt forward in open-topped holsters designed for a fast cavalry twist-hand draw.

In the days when he rode as first lieutenant of Company C, Red Blaze gained a reputation for being hotheaded and with a penchant for becoming involved in fights. Not that he was a troublemaker, but fights seemed to come his way with the persistence of iron filings being drawn to a magnet. Nothing in his career since the end of the war, including his marriage over in Arizona, showed a change in his ways. Maybe Red acted a mite more subdued, but he still managed to find more than his fair share of any fuss going in his vicinity.

Before Sandy could raise any further comment on Red Blaze's changed state caused by matrimony, another of the guests joined the conversation.

"Billy Jack keeping you-all happied up, Sandy?"

The speaker had been Sandy's commanding officer and was the man claimed by many to be the best fighting cavalry leader produced by either side during the war. In fact, his handling of Company C on the Arkansas battlefront gave the Yankees a foretaste of the kind of fighting they would later meet when dealing with the hostile Indians of the West.

Among a crowd where the average height was six feet, the speaker could easily have passed unnoticed. Five feet six at most, he seemed small and insignificant. Dressed in good-quality range clothes, he gave them the appearance of cast-aside hand-downs, and not even the matched bone-handled 1860 Army Colts riding butt forward in well-tooled cross-draw holsters made him more noticeable. Yet not one of the men around him gave thought to his lack of inches, nor did they overlook him. His name was Dusty Fog.

Although small, Dusty did not look puny. He had width to his shoulders that hinted at the strength of a pocket Hercules. Dusty blond hair showed from under his thrust-back black

J. B. Stetson hat. Handsome, though not eye-catchingly so, his face showed humor, strength of will, intelligence, all hinting at the true man beneath the small exterior. No man who saw Dusty Fog in a dangerous situation ever thought of him in mere feet and inches again.

With the end of the war Dusty prepared to forget his distinguished career as a soldier, despite General Grant's offer that he be transferred to the Union Army retaining rank and seniority, in favor of helping to retrieve the great OD Connected ranch from five years of neglect caused by shortage of manpower. Things did not work out the way he planned. Sent on a mission of vital importance to the peace of the United States, he went into strife-torn Mexico and returned successful, bringing back two good friends, with whom, together with Red Blaze, he planned to form a floating outfit for the ranch. Although a floating outfit was normally a group of cowhands who worked as a kind of mobile ranch crew on the spread's farthest ranges, Dusty and his companions found themselves employed more and more to help friends of their boss out of difficulties.

During the years between the disbanding of the Texas Light Cavalry and the night of Sandy McGraw's bachelor party Dusty Fog built up quite a name for himself as cowhand of the top grade, trail boss equal to the best, peace officer of high ability, and, aided by a knowledge of Oriental fighting methods gained from Ole Devil Hardin's Japanese servant, fistfighter par excellence. Mainly, however, Texans spoke of his amazing skill and inimitable speed when using that pair of Army Colts, claiming him to be the fastest and most accurate of all the *pistolero* experts war or Reconstruction produced in the Lone Star State.

All in all, Sandy felt pleased that his old commander found time to attend the wedding. After helping persuade the majority of the Comanche bands to give up their old way of life, sign a peace treaty, and move onto reservations, Dusty took time out to accompany Red as a wedding guest. Neither of the other members of the floating outfit managed to come along, Mark Counter having ridden off to help protect a wounded uncle from a bunch of vicious killers, and the Ysabel Kid having stopped on at Fort Sorrel to handle the final details of resettling the Pehnane band of the Comanches on their new home.

"He sure was, Cap'n." Sandy grinned in answer to Dusty's question. "Been telling me what a fine piece of land I've got."

"It's good range, or so I've heard," Dusty admitted. "Have you got everything fixed for going there?"

"Near enough. I have to be there by the tenth to pay off Uncle Seth's last year's taxes, and the place's mine."

"Taxes?"

"Five hundred dollars, payable afore noon on the tenth or the place goes up for public auction."

"Can you manage it?"

"Easy enough, Cap'n. Sarah and me's fixing to leave here day after tomorrow, and that'll give us plenty of time to reach San Garcia afore the tenth."

"If you need anything—" Dusty began.

"Nope," Sandy replied. "Thanks anyways, Cap'n. Sarah and me'll get by. We saved enough to pay off the taxes and leave some to live on until the spread starts to keep us."

"Sure. But Uncle Devil says for you to let us know happen you need help."

That was typical of Ole Devil Hardin. The late commanding general of the Confederate Army of Arkansas did not forget the men whose courage and loyalty had helped him hold back the superior, in arms and numbers, Federal forces in the Bear State. Crippled in an attempt to ride the huge paint stallion Dusty Fog later tamed and used as his personal mount, Ole Devil could not make the trip to San Antonio. So he sent his ranch's *segundo,* his granddaughter, and a member of his floating outfit to act as his representatives. He also offered any assistance that the newly wedded couple might need during the early days of the married life.

"Hey, Cap'n Dusty!" called one of the crowd. "You're not drinking."

"I'm doing what I call drinking," Dusty answered with a grin and caught the bartender's eye. "Fill them up again, Stormy."

"Yo!" came the old cavalry reply.

There might be bigger, more lavish saloons in San Antonio, but the Bull's Head belonged to Stormy Weather, who once wore three stripes in Company C and by virtue of that offered an ideal venue for Sandy McGraw's last fling as a bachelor. Working fast, Stormy refilled glasses and then settled back to watch his wartime companions enjoying themselves.

All around stood men with a common bond of dangers shared, gathered together for a celebration and indulging in the kind of small talk one might expect on such an occasion. After disbanding, the members of Company C spread across Texas in search of a new life, and meeting like this set off a chain of reminiscence, prompted inquiries as to the whereabouts of absent friends, spawned tall stories, or caused old battles to be refought. To one side the cattle industry was being discussed, various comments being passed on the subject of prices, predators, diseases, and all the other aspects that meant the success or failure of Texas's major business. By the saloon's battered piano, some of the party raised their voices in song, which sometimes was in key with the jangling notes.

Leaning his elbow on the bar, Red Blaze took everything in, and a feeling of content wore down the nagging twinge of conscience that bothered him. While helping hunt down a stock-killing cougar on the OD Connected, his wife took a fall from her horse. Born and raised on a ranch, Sue Blaze landed without serious injury but managed to twist her ankle badly. Red wanted to stay with her, for the injury prevented Sue from walking, but she insisted that he attend the wedding. Knowing she would be in good hands, Red reluctantly agreed to make the trip. For all that, he felt just a touch disturbed at the thought of leaving Sue behind.

"Hey, Red," said a man, "you hear about Sam Jackley? He's driving a stage for Wells Fargo up Houston way now."

"He always was a good driver," Red answered, coming out of his reverie.

"Sure. Well, seems like this old gal come up just afore he was pulling out on his run, and she'd got just about the meanest, orneriest hound dawg a man ever did see with her. Naturally Sam tells her she's not taking that fool dawg on his stage. Anyways, they argues back and forward a piece until Sam gets the mail aboard and takes up the ribbons. 'All right!' the old gal shouts. 'You know what you can do with your stage' and Sam says right back, 'Sure, ma'am. And happen you can do it with your old hound dawg, you can get on for the ride.' "

Red chuckled, and the man ambled on to try his story out upon some other member of the party. Sipping at his drink, Red listened to snatches of conversation taking place around him.

"Mind that time we charged the Yankee Napoleons on the Snake Ford of the Ouachita, when the Arkansas Rifles were given them false orders to take it—"

"And Tom's ole woman done figured to give him a pleasant surprise seeing's he'd just come back off the trail. So she gets on her fanciest nightgown, puts some perfume and face fixings on, and goes into the bedroom. 'Darling,' she says. 'It's your wife.' Well, sir, ole Tom jumps out of bed and yells, 'For the Lord's sake, hide me, *pronto*!' "

"If you go to Abilene, watch that bastard Hickok. Man, he'd shoot you in the head as soon as look at you, or maybe sooner."

"Cap'n Dusty sure made Wyatt Earp sing low when he took that Rocking H trail herd to Dodge after Earp said it hadn't to go there."

"I wouldn't say Benny picked the smartest gal in town. Fact being there's times—Why, he done took home a turkey he'd shot, and at dinner next day he says, 'What'd you stuff this old bird with, gal?' And she says, 'Stuff it? I didn't know it was hollow.' "

"And I says it was Kiowa riding scout that day—"

> A rancher riding home one night,
> Did find his house without a light,
> And as he lit a match to go to bed,
> A sudden thought came to his head.

Clearly the choice of song by the group around the piano did not please a bunch standing at the other end of the bar, for they cut loose in opposition.

Once there was a maiden a-sweeping with a broom,
Had to undo her apron's strings to give her belly room,
Her father looked upon her and whispered in her ear,
"Oh, tell me what you've got beneath your apron."

"It's sure a pity Mark and the Kid couldn't make it, Red,"
Stormy Weather commented after serving the customers. "This
looks like their kind of fun."

"It sure does." Red grinned. "Now iffen we could only have
somebody come in that we didn't like—"

"No, thank you 'most to death. I've just got this place started
and don't want its fixings busting."

"I mind the time when you was the first one to start the
fussing, Stormy," Red pointed out.

"That was *afore* I bought my own place," Weather replied,
and turned to look along the counter. "All right, all right. You
won't die of thirst afore I reach you. Or if you do, you'll be the
wettest thirsty jasper in this room."

Watching the saloonkeeper move off to attend to business,
Red finished his drink and set the glass down. Listening to the
noise around him, he felt at peace with the world. Sandy's
bachelor party appeared to be going fine. Of course, a real good
fistfight would sure spark it up and make for a memorable
night, but Stormy Weather had just started the saloon going
and must not have his capital eaten up repairing damage caused
by a brawl.

"Maybe I ought to ask him who takes most of his trade and
go down there to see what's doing," Red mused with a grin.
"Whooee! Wouldn't that Sue gal of mine rake my hide happen I
did and wound up in jail?"

Reluctantly Red put aside thoughts of enjoying a real rough-
house, relegating it along with other bachelor pursuits to those
unfortunates who had not yet embraced the benefits of matrimony. Of course, if somebody came in looking for fuss . . .

Thrusting himself away from the bar, Red passed among the
crowd and made a leisurely way across the room. By the time
he reached the building's front entrance he felt the need for a
breath of fresh air, for the room's atmosphere had grown heavy

with tobacco smoke, because of the larger than capacity crowd present. Pushing open the batwing doors, he stepped through and onto the sidewalk.

Idly glancing across the street, Red saw a couple of men standing in the alley between the two business premises—both closed and darkened for the night—opposite the saloon. At first he figured them to be no more than a couple of loafers attracted by the sound of revelry and wondering how they might join it. Then his instincts screamed out a warning. Red had taken a few drinks but not enough to dull his perceptions or spoil his faculties. So he saw and understood the significant manner in which one of the pair stood. Nor did he need to observe the dull metallic glint stretching from the man's hand to realize his own position.

An instant before flame spurted from the raised hand of the man across the street, Red went forward in a rolling dive that carried him through the patch of light thrown by the batwing doors and off the sidewalk. Lead made its eerie *splat!* sound as it burst through the air above Red, where his body had been so short a time before. Then he landed in the welcome blackness provided by the angle of the raised sidewalk.

While falling, Red twisted his right-hand palm out to coil fingers around the walnut grips of his offside Colt. Smoothly he slid the gun's streamlined length from leather, thumb-cocking its single-action mechanism in the process and slipping the forefinger into the trigger guard when the eight-inch barrel slanted away from him. Red could not claim to be fast with a gun, taking slightly over a second to draw and shoot when a real *fast* man could halve that time, but he still held a gun ready for use when he lit down on the ground.

For all that, Red did not throw lead indiscriminately at his unknown assailants. Instead he watched them as he fell and took quick sight along the Colt's barrel after he landed. The 1860 Army Colt could claim to be one of the best fighting handguns made, comparatively light in weight yet offering a sufficiently heavy caliber to knock down and take the fight out of an enemy with one shot, but its construction did not make for fancy target-shooting accuracy. To be fair, the Army Colt had been designed with the needs of sedentary eastern target poppers in mind, being produced as a fighting weapon that suited the requirements of cavalry soldiers and others who needed a means of defense while riding a horse.

With his aim taken, Red squeezed the Colt's trigger, saw the hammer swing around to strike the waiting percussion cap, and felt the recoil buck as the gas caused by suddenly burning black powder thrust a conical bullet through the barrel. Muzzle blast flared redly from the Colt and momentarily blinded Red with its glow, but he heard a screech from across the street following on the unmistakable *whomp!* a bullet made when it smashed into living tissue.

On firing, Red rolled two complete turns to the left. Startled by the shots, the horses tied to the hitching rail moved and reared restlessly. Steel-shod hooves struck the ground close by Red, and he lay without movement. Rolling had been a wise precaution, along with his choice of the direction he rolled. Red might be hotheaded and liable to plunge into any fight he saw without too close inquiry as to its cause, but once in, he became a cool enough hand, thinking out his moves with lightning speed.

Fully aware of how burning powder threw out a glow in the darkness, he knew the men across the street could easily mark his position when he fired. If they possessed even a small knowledge of gunfighting, the pair—or its uninjured number— ought to guess that he would not stay put after throwing the shot. Red also figured his assailants would expect him to roll away from the horses and so did the opposite, chancing a stamp or kick as preferable to receiving a bullet. When a second shot thundered from across the street and its bullet thudded into the sidewalk to the right of his original position, Red knew he had called the play correctly.

Having automatically recocked his Colt after firing, Red prepared to use it again. He waited for his eyes to throw off the effects of the muzzle blast, knowing that the next bullet must put his second attacker out of action. There could be only one way for him to roll should he fire again, for if he went farther to the left, he would be under the nearest horse. That meant his adversary across the street knew the direction in which he must move and could aim accordingly, given the chance.

Even as Red's eyes cleared, he heard significant sounds from the building behind him and the thud of departing feet across the street.

Now who the hell'd want to kill sweet, lovable lil ole me? he wondered while staying on the ground and awaiting developments.

2

Nine months later a baby boy was born,
Born without a pappy in this wicked world of scorn.
Her father looked upon her, and he whispered in her ear,
"Now I know what you had beneath your apron!"

The second group of singers had gained ascendancy, and practically the whole of the room joined in, roaring out the words lustily. Then the sound of shots cut over their voices and brought a sudden, shocked hush. Probably Dusty alone had noticed Red's departure, but all the rest knew there was trouble afoot. Even the knowledge of Red's love of practical jokes did not cause Dusty to lay a wrong interpretation on the shots. Sure, Red liked to stir up fun, but not of the stupid kind involving the reckless discharging of a gun. In any case, two of the shots had come from across the street.

In that moment Dusty showed what made him a leader of men despite his lack of inches. Long before any of the others could put thoughts to words, he reached his decision and barked out orders.

"Billy Jack, left door. Stan, right door. Tracey, right window, Vic, left. Kiowa, come with me."

Even as he spoke, Dusty headed for the front door and slid the left-hand Colt from his holster on his right side. Celebrations were forgotten, and the men sobered up fast as they sprang to obey their leader's orders. Reaching the front of the building, Dusty did not dash straight out. Instead he flattened himself against the wall alongside and peered over the top of the batwing doors. A glance at the tall, lean Kiowa told Dusty that the company's scout was ready to play his part. Suddenly Dusty thrust himself through the doors, sprang across the patch of light to the left, and halted in the flimsy protection of the porch's upright cover support. An instant later Kiowa repeated Dusty's move but went to the right.

No bullets came their way, although the manner in which they acted was designed to confuse the enemy and make him unsure of which to shoot at first. Swiftly Dusty raked the opposite side of the street with his eyes. At first he thought it to be deserted, then saw a shape sprawled on the ground.

"Are you all right, Cousin Red?" he asked.

"Sure, Cousin Dusty. I hit one, and the other ran."

"Where was he?"

"Across the street, between the saddler's shop and the hardware store."

"You hear that, Billy Jack, Stan?" Dusty called, having heard enough to tell him the flanking parties had reached their assigned positions.

"I heard," Billy Jack assured Dusty.

"We're watching 'em real good, even if we can't see 'em, Cap'n Dusty," the man at the other end of the saloon said.

"Let's go over and say howdy then, Cousin Red!" Dusty ordered.

"I thought you'd never ask," Red drawled, and came to his feet.

Placing his right hand on the hitching rail, Dusty vaulted over it and landed by his cousin. With Kiowa at the other side,

Dusty headed across the street toward the still shape in the alley. Although running, the trio kept their revolvers ready for use. Nor did the sight of the gun lying close by the sprawled-out man cause them to relax or regret taking precautions.

"Get after the other one, Kiowa!" Dusty barked, knowing that aspect of the work could best be handled by the scout.

Silently Kiowa faded off down the alley, keeping in the darkest shadows and moving with the soft-footed skill of his red forefathers. Alert and ready to deal with any attempted move the other might make, Dusty and Red approached the shot man. Kicking the gun farther away from the still hand, Dusty moved closer and sank to a knee. He rasped a match taken from his pocket on the seat of his pants, and its glow illuminated an unshaven, lean face twisted in agony, the glazed eyes staring blindly.

"Know him, Cousin Red?"

"I've never seen him before that I can recall," Red replied, holstering his Colt and studying the body; his assailant was dead, caught in the left side of the chest by the bullet, which ranged on through the heart.

Men crowded out of the saloon, joining the flanking parties as they converged on where Dusty knelt by the body. Tossing aside the spent match, Dusty took another from his pocket. Before he could strike it, Kiowa returned.

"He's gone, Cap'n Dusty," the scout reported. "Couldn't hear him going neither. You want for me to take some of the boys and look around?"

"San Antonio's a fair-sized city," Dusty pointed out. "Which same that jasper'll be long gone afore you can find him."

"The great seizer's coming, Cap'n Dusty," Billy Jack put in dismally, although he knew Town Marshal Anse Dale to be a friend.

Hearing the shooting while making his rounds, Dale drew the correct conclusion. He knew that none of the assembled members of Company C was the kind to shoot off guns in the street for fun and so came to investigate. After passing through the crowd, he halted and looked down.

"You, Dusty?" he asked, indicating the body.

"Red," the small Texan replied.

"Figure you had a good reason for it, Red," the marshal stated.

"There's some might not call it that, but I reckon I had," Red replied. "Him and his pard took a shot at me as I came out of the Bull's Head."

"Is there any reason why they should?"

"If there is, I'm damned if I know it, Anse."

"Who is he?" the marshal wanted to know.

"Can't say that I've ever seen him before," Red replied. "Not that I had a good look, mind."

"Maybe you'll know him, Anse," Dusty remarked, glancing to where Weather came from the saloon with a lit lantern in hand. "Let's have some light over here, Stormy."

With the better illumination afforded by the lantern, Red studied the dead man's face more carefully. Bending down, Dale also looked at the unshaven features and then turned his eyes to Red.

"How about it?"

"Like I said, I've never seen this jasper before," Red stated.

"Have you, Anse?" asked Dusty.

"Nope, but I don't get to see every drifter who comes into town."

"Hey, though!" Weather interjected, moving by Dusty and bending down. "I've seen him afore."

"Where?" Dusty demanded.

Maybe the marshal should have asked the questions, but in addition to riding for the OD Connected, Red was Dusty's kin, and the small Texan felt very interested in the reason for the attempted killing. Certainly Dale raised no objection to Dusty's usurping his official position.

"In my place earlier," Weather replied. "Him and another feller were there."

"Did they ask about Red or show any interest in him?"

"No, Cap'n. Just asked what the party was for, and I told them we was sending Sandy off afore the marrying."

"Talking about that," the marshal remarked, glancing around him, "why don't you boys go back to your drinking and carousing? Stormy's not making any money off you while you're out here."

"I didn't know you cared, Anse." The saloonkeeper grinned.

"I for sure do," Dale insisted. "If you don't make money, you can't pay your civic taxes. Which same if they don't get paid, the town can't afford to pay me, and I might even have to go back to work."

"There's none of us'd want *that,*" Dusty drawled, sweeping a cold eye at the gathered men. "Just take a quick look and see if any of you know him, then go help pay Dale's wages. The cattle business's just getting back on its feet, and we don't want him to come back to being a cow nurse."

Although various members of the crowd came from different parts of the state, not one of them could offer any hint to the dead man's identity. After each man had expressed his ignorance, he headed back to the light and hospitality of the saloon. At last only Dusty, Red, and Dale remained by the body. Even the small knot of San Antonio's citizens who gathered at the scene of the drama failed to give any light to the matter and withdrew when sure nothing further would develop. Quickly Dale went through the man's pockets, studying his findings in the light of the lantern before dropping them into the hat that had come off when its wearer struck the ground.

"Only the usual stuff," he said at the end of the search. "Thirty dollars, the makings, handkerchief. Nothing to say who he is or why he's here."

"You didn't think he'd have a letter telling him to come here and make a try at killing Cousin Red, did you?" Dusty drawled.

"There's always the odd chance he might," Dale answered. "How about it, Red? Do you have any ideas why they tried to kill you?"

"Could be they figured there'd be the chance of robbing some of us when we come drunk and careless from the wingding," Red replied. "And afore you tell me, that doesn't explain why this jasper started throwing lead as soon as I came out."

"Have you got any enemies?" asked Dale, suggesting the most obvious cause for a murder attempt.

"Me?" yelped Red in surprise. "Hell, no!"

Despite his way of becoming involved in fights, Red rarely made a lasting enemy. Possessed of a friendly nature, he mostly won over his opponents once the fists had stopped flying and frequently wound up on the best of terms with them. So he could not think of a single person who might want to see him dead. Certainly not to the extent of hiring strangers to do the killing.

"If you'd been dressed different, I'd say maybe they made a mistake and picked the wrong man," Dale commented.

"What's wrong with how I'm dressed?" Red demanded indignantly.

"Not a thing." The marshal grinned. "Only with that red hair and bandanna you'd take a heap of missing."

"Across the width of the street and in the dark?" Red sniffed.

"You'd just come through the light at the door," Dusty pointed out. "And even if they couldn't make out your hair or that bandanna, they for sure couldn't miss the vest. There's not another like it in the room."

"If there had been, I'd've whipped the feller wearing it," Red stated. "I'll have you know this here vest's much admired by folks with taste and discernment."

"Which same I can well believe," said Dale. "Only it sure catches the eye. Those pair was after you for certain sure, Red."

"I can't think why," Red told the listening pair. "Now if it was Cousin Dusty they were after, I could understand it."

"Are you saying I'm not popular, Cousin?" Dusty demanded.

"Shucks, no. It's only that you don't have my pleasing nature and winning ways, Dusty. How about it, Anse, you fixing to slap me in the pokey over this?"

"The day I have to jail a man for defending hisself I'll go back to nursing cows and to hell with ruining the cattle business!" snorted Dale.

"Let's go on back inside, Red," Dusty suggested.

"How about if this one's pard comes back and makes another try?" asked the marshal.

"Let him try it," Red growled. "We'll see if we can take him alive. I'd sure like to talk to him."

"Tell you what I'll do," Dale drawled. "I'll come in and ask Stormy what the other jasper looks like and then send my deputies around town to see if they can find any sign of him."

"If you need any extra deputies—" Dusty began.

"If you reckon I'm turning that bunch loose on my town, you're plumb loco, Dusty." Dale grinned, nodding in the direction of the saloon. "They'd take it apart board by board was you to tell 'em. Leave it to my boys, and you fellers have your fun out."

"Sure, Anse. I'll be here happen you learn anything. And I'd admire to talk to that jasper if you lay hands on him."

"Me, too," Red put in. "Leave us not forget I was the one they shot at."

"If Cousin Betty happened to hear the shooting and comes asking what's going on, Anse," Dusty remarked as they started across the street toward the saloon, "tell her it was just the boys horsing around."

"Will she believe it?" the marshal grinned, knowing Miss Betty Hardin pretty well.

"Nope," admitted Dusty. "But she'll act like she does and give us hell when she sees us in the morning."

"Anyways," Red stated as they reached the batwing doors of the Bull's Head, "I bet that jasper's long gone out of town by now."

Although none of them knew it, Red guessed wrongly about the would-be killer's actions and whereabouts.

While flight did cross Paco Murphy's mind when he saw the ambush fail and Talbot go down, his greed caused him to change his mind. The man who had hired him had paid only a small advance, insisting on the work's being brought to a successful conclusion before handing over the full payment. Having put some time and effort into the chore so far, he decided to take a chance on finishing what he started. That damned redhead could not have recognized Murphy across the width of the street or be able to describe him. Nor would Talbot lead the

law or vengeance-seeking members of Company C to Murphy.
They had never worked together before; in fact, Murphy took
on Talbot only when he learned the kind of company his victim
would be keeping that night. Unless Murphy guessed badly
wrong, Talbot could not talk. A man did not easily forget the
sound a bullet made when it drove into a human chest. No, sir,
Talbot lay either dead or too badly hurt to talk back there, and
likely the other folks involved believed Murphy to be acting as
would any sensible man who made an attempt at killing a
friend of Dusty Fog. Possibly there would be no other chance
to earn his pay that night, but if he stayed on, a further opportunity might present itself in the confusion of the wedding.

Once clear of the Bull's Head saloon's immediate area, Murphy slowed his pace to a walk as being less likely to draw
attention to himself. He also quit the back streets and swung
onto the sidewalk to stroll down in the direction of the Casa
Moreno Hotel. It might not be the best place in town, but he
could merge into its crowd and attract little attention.

Ignoring the main entrance, Murphy pushed open the batwing doors of the hotel's barroom and stepped inside. Business
appeared to be slack that night, the only other customers being
a trio of young townsmen who stood examining a fair-sized
wicker basket on the bar before them. Even as Murphy thought
of withdrawing, the bartender looked up from his study of a
tattered copy of the *Police Gazette* and eyed him appraisingly.

The bartender saw a stocky man of medium height, wearing
range clothes, with an Allen & Wheelock Army revolver in a
tied-down holster and a knife's hilt rising from the top of his
left boot. Studying the sombrero, as opposed to the more usual
Stetson, charro jacket, frilly-fronted shirt, string tie, the bartender concluded his latest customer hailed from down on the
Rio Grande. An olive-skinned face that looked like a mixture
of Irish and Mexican told of mixed blood. Maybe somebody
from the East might have taken Murphy for a cowboy, but not
the range-wise bartender. Any cattle work that hard-eyed cuss
did would not be for the owner of the animals, and his main
source of income most likely came by that gun from which his
right hand rarely strayed too far.

Deciding that to turn and walk out again might attract too much attention, Murphy strolled across to the bar.

"You're quiet in here tonight," he commented.

"You're here a day too soon," the bartender replied. "The cock- and snakefights aren't until tomorrow night."

Despite wearing his particular style of clothing, Murphy disliked any hint about his mixed blood. So he scowled at the words and their implication. While some white men attended the snake- or cockfights arranged by the hotel's owner, the majority of the audience was Mexican. Before he could raise the point, Murphy heard something that took his thoughts from the bartender.

"One more drink, and then we'll go give Sarah her wedding present," announced the tall, sullenly handsome young man in the center of the trio, slapping his right hand on the wicker basket's lid. "When she opens it up, she'll screech the house down."

Immediately Murphy became all interest, although he did not show it. To the best of his knowledge, there was only one wedding due around San Antonio in the near future, that between Sandy McGraw and Sarah Maybelle.

"This'll teach her to throw you over for that damned cow nurse, Chester," declared the burly German-looking young man at the first speaker's right side.

"When them horned toads start hopping out, squirting blood from their eyes, that bridal shower'll be the rowdiest this town's ever seen," said the third of the party, a slightly younger version of the second.

"Damned fools," the bartender sniffed, directing a scorn-filled glance at the trio and speaking to Murphy. "Chester Finwald there was sparking Sarah Maybelle. Only she picked Sandy McGraw from out to the Flying O, fact being they're getting hitched tomorrow. So Chester's been drowning his sorrows."

"We'll put the basket on the porch and leave it there," Finwald told his companions. "Sooner or later somebody'll find it and take it in."

"I'd like to see their faces when they open it." Fritz Soehnen grinned. "What say we hang around outside—"

"Naw!" his elder brother, Hans, sniffed. "If we get seen, Sandy McGraw'll set all his pards on to us."

"Where'd a man go, happen he wants to go?" Murphy asked the bartender.

"Out the back there."

Leaving the barroom, Murphy walked along a passage that he knew led to the rear entrance. His memory of an earlier visit served him well, for he saw a sign reading KEEP OUT—DANGER pinned to one of the doors siding the passage. After a quick glance around to make sure he was unobserved, Murphy tried the door's handle. After easing the door open, he entered and went down a flight of stairs into the large cellar that spread beneath the building. In the center was the large, sloping-sided pit used for snake- or cockfights, but he ignored it. His attention went to two lines of wicker baskets standing alongside the far wall. After crossing the cellar, he tapped the first basket of one pile, studying it in the light of the hanging lamps. Only a rustling sound answered him, so he went to the second pile and repeated the tap. This time a harsh, staccato buzzing greeted the tap, and he nodded in satisfaction. His assumption that the proprietor would have already gathered the snakes for the fights proved correct. After taking up the basket, he returned to the cellar door, eased it open, and peered out.

Nor did Murphy appear a moment too soon. Laughing, talking, and jostling one another, the trio of young men passed out the rear door as he emerged from the cellar. Certain that nobody had seen him enter or leave the cellar, Murphy followed on their heels.

Unaware of the man's presence, Finwald and the Soehnen brothers strolled along the rear streets. Murphy dogged their footsteps, keeping far enough back to remain unobserved but close enough to make sure he knew which way they headed. At last the trio halted before a small house in the better part of the working-class residential area. While the brothers waited, Finwald opened the picket fence's gate and sneaked along the path to set down his basket on the porch. Only the sitting room at the front showed a light, and female laughter sounded from inside its curtained-over windows. Returning to his companions, Finwald grinned, and they faded off into the darkness.

As soon as the trio departed, Murphy approached the gate. With even more caution than Finwald showed, the man stalked up to the house. He set down the basket and reached toward the other. Then he saw the piece of paper fixed on the lid of Finwald's basket. After taking off the paper, he transferred it to the other basket. When the law came around, that paper's written message ought to lead it off on a false scent. Holding Finwald's basket, Murphy eased the other up to the door. Then he gave a tug at the bellpull and, as it started to clang, withdrew to beyond the picket fence. Taking cover behind a tree, he saw a girl open the door and look out. After picking up the basket, she entered the house. As the door closed, Murphy turned and walked away. He tossed aside Finwald's basket, not wanting to be found with anything so incriminating, and continued on his way, hoping that he might have more success this time with the job for which he had been hired.

3

Although the bridal shower appeared to be going down well, Sarah Maybelle wondered if one of her guests might not find it dull and boring. A dozen of her friends filled the sitting room, laughing, talking, and examining the presents with every indication of pleasure, and Sarah failed to detect any other signs on the face of Betty Hardin.

Darting a glance at the small, petite, beautiful Betty, Sarah wondered what the other really thought of the affair. Of course, the black-haired girl was far too well bred to criticize openly, but there might be adverse thoughts underneath the smiling face and behind the black, alert eyes. Granddaughter of one of Texas's richest men, Betty had traveled extensively and on occasion mingled on equal terms with some of the most important people in the state. She might find a small-town bridal shower a dull affair, the conversation of its guests boring after the witty talk heard at her usual kind of party.

Sarah did not need to worry, for Betty felt none of the sentiments the bride-to-be suspected. Associating with the richest in the land did not prevent Betty from enjoying the simple and gentle pleasure of watching a girl open up such wedding gifts as friends and relatives could afford. One of Betty's greatest assets had always been her ability to enjoy any company in which she found herself. No snob, she did not look down on the other girls present because their parents lacked her family's wealth and social standing. At first the other guests tended to be shy; but she broke down their barriers, and the bridal shower became as lively as such an affair ought to be.

Hearing the sound of the door's bell, an innovation fitted by Sarah's father and much admired by the neighbors, one of the girls left the room. She returned carrying a wicker basket that she set on the table.

"Who was it?" Sarah asked.

"An unknown admirer," the girl replied, and indicated the piece of paper.

Reaching out her hand, the middle-sized, pretty brunette bride-to-be freed the paper and read it with a frown.

" 'Guess who?' " she read.

"Open it up, Sarah," suggested a big blond girl with a slight Swedish accent.

"I suppose I may as well," Sarah replied, and drew free the pin that secured the lid. "Although I never thought he'd se—"

While speaking, the girl lifted the lid. A startled gasp broke from her lips, almost drowned by the vicious buzz of an angry rattlesnake. Seeing the light, the snake began to rear up. Its neck curved into an S shape, and the evil-looking, flat, triangular head with its curved three-quarters-of-an-inch-long fangs rose. All the time the snake's tail vibrated the numerous interconnected horny caps to blast out the warning rattle that gave *Crotalus horridus* its common name.

Something about Sarah's attitude had triggered off a warning alarm inside Betty Hardin. On hearing the first wicked buzz from the basket, the girl realized the nature of its contents. Lunging across the table, Betty slammed down the basket's lid. Fast though she moved, the snake had already raised its head clear, and the closing lid caught it across the neck. Desperately

Betty held the lid down, feeling the muscular power of the trapped snake as it thrashed around inside.

"Open the window, quickly!" she snapped.

Every girl in the room had been raised in frontier Texas. So although the snake's appearance shocked and scared them, it did not induce complete panic. Sarah staggered backward and sat down hard on the floor, but the big blonde sprang to obey Betty's order. After throwing open the window and jerking apart its curtains, the blonde moved aside and stared back across the room.

Gripping the basket with all her strength, Betty raised it from the table and held it at arm's length. Slowly she started to walk toward the window with her burden. Inside the basket the snake thrashed its length into rage-filled knots and made the room vibrate with its furious buzzing. Betty held on grimly, stepping as if walking on eggshells. If the basket fell from her grasp, the raging snake would be free to attack the girls around it.

Sweat trickled down Betty's face, getting into her eyes, and the memory of something an imported female tutor told her as a child sprang idiotically to mind.

"Servants sweat," the tutor used to recite. "Gentlemen perspire, but ladies only glow."

Which means I'm no lady, Betty mused. *Because, lordy lord, I'm sure sweating up a storm. Or if I'm glowing, it's the wettest glow I ever saw.*

By that time she had reached the window and could put aside the fantasies that helped prevent her from thinking of the fate awaiting her should she drop the basket. No matter whom else the snake struck, it was sure to nail her as the closest person to it on regaining its freedom.

Sucking in a deep breath, Betty heaved the basket through the open window. She saw it strike the porch rail and start to tip. Instantly the snake erupted, landed on the rail, then flopped into the garden. The buzzing ended, and Betty fancied she could hear the snake whizzing through Mrs. Maybelle's flowers as it headed for the open range. Imagination was all it could be, for Ilsa Swenson jerked down the open window the instant after Betty had evicted the snake-filled basket, moving with such smooth precision that they might have been practicing together for years.

"I am *not* sweating; it's only a ladylike glow," Betty gasped, flopping her back against the wall.

"What?" asked Ilsa.

"Did I say something?" Betty inquired, realizing that she must have spoken her thoughts aloud.

Then she looked around at the strained faces of the other girls. Strained maybe, but one held a poker grabbed up from the fireplace, and another stood holding Mr. Maybelle's shotgun, which she had taken from the deerhorn hooks on the wall.

"Was it a joke?" inquired another of the guests, helping Sarah to her feet.

"If it was, I can't say much for San Antonio humor," Betty said before the hostess could answer. "Do you know who sent it, Sarah?"

"I—I—"

Sensing that the girl knew but did not wish to divulge the sender's name before her friends, Betty moved from the wall. Dabbing her face with a lace handkerchief, she looked pointedly around.

"All that excitement has sure given me an appetite."

"And me," Lisa said, either because she caught Betty's glance or through genuine hunger. "Let's raid the kitchen. Come on, girls."

Sarah's parents had gone to visit with friends, leaving the girls alone in the house, so, aware that they would not be disturbing anybody, Lisa herded the others from the sitting room. When Sarah started to follow her friends, Betty caught her by the arm and halted her.

"Who sent it?" Betty demanded.

"I—I'm not sure."

"Then guess!"

"I don't want to get Che—anybody into trouble. It was only a joke."

"Some joke!" Betty snapped. "That was a rattler, not a harmless king snake. Just take a look there!"

Following the direction in which Betty pointed, Sarah saw two large spots of liquid staining the tablecloth where the basket had been. A shudder ran through the brunette's frame as she realized that the liquid must have splashed from the snake's poison-squirting fangs.

"Oh, Betty!" she gasped. "If Pa or Sandy hear about this—"

"There's no way we can stop them from hearing," Betty pointed out.

"But there'll be trouble—"

"That's for sure," Betty said grimly. "And I want to make certain it's under control when it comes."

"I don't want anybody to get hurt," Sarah objected.

"Listen, honey," Betty said gently, taking the brunette's hand, "I know how you feel. But this can't be just dropped. Whoever did it might pull another fool game, and this time somebody could get hurt bad. That somebody might even be Sandy. Whoever sent you that snake may try the same on him."

Something of a student of human nature, Betty used an argument she felt sure would make Sarah change her feelings on the matter. An expression of concern flickered across the brunette's face, and she stared at the two splashes of poison upon the table.

"I recognize the writing. It's Chester Finwald's."

"You're sure of it?"

"Yes. He used to come courting me before I met Sandy, and I've seen his writing plenty of times."

"Did he object to you dropping him for Sandy?" Betty asked.

"Well—yes, he did. Not that we'd ever been serious," Sarah replied. "In fact, he and Sandy got to fighting one night at a dance and Sandy licked him. What're you going to do, Betty?"

The question came as Betty started to turn from the table.

"Go and tell Cousin Dusty what's happened. Will you ask one of your friends to show me the way to the Bull's Head saloon, please?"

"Do you have to tell him?"

"Listen, Sarah," Betty said gently, "this may have been no more than a stupid joke on Finwald's part, but you could easily have been killed. If Sandy hears about it, I can't see him taking it kindly. Now I don't know what kind of man this Finwald is, but Sandy's pretty good with a gun. You don't want a shooting before the wedding, and it might easily come to that."

"I suppose so." Sarah sighed. "But if you ask me, it was those Soehnen boys who put Chester up to it. He's been hanging around with them a lot recently. Shall I go with you?"

"No. I'd rather one of the other girls did."

Sarah left the room and returned with the big blonde. "Ilsa says she'll go with you, Betty."

"We'd better go the back way," Ilsa remarked. "That way nobody will see us go to the saloon."

"It would be best." Betty smiled.

Not wishing to make the other guests uncomfortable or appear to be flaunting her superior social standing, Betty had attended the bridal shower in a plain, neat black traveling suit and white blouse. It would serve admirably for walking through the back streets. She carried a Remington double derringer in her reticule and could handle it well enough to make any would-be joker regret his actions if the need arose.

"Shall we go, Ilsa?" Betty asked, and looked at Sarah. "Don't worry, Cousin Dusty will see everything's put right. But don't open any more mysterious presents if they come."

While Betty agreed with Ilsa's suggestion of keeping to the back streets, the precaution did not entirely succeed. At first they walked along without meeting anybody. Then a tall young cowhand lurched from a side alley in front of them. One glance told Betty that he carried a fair load of Old Stump Blaster internally, enough to make him feel amorous. Halting, he surveyed the two girls in a satisfied manner, beamed delightedly, and teetered toward them.

"I bet you gals're looking for me," he announced, blocking their path.

"You'd lose," Betty replied tolerantly.

"Well, now, I'd surely admire to take you-all where you're going."

"Some other time, maybe," Betty told him, and started to walk by.

"They do say there's no time like the present, lil gal," the cowhand replied, turning and hooking his left arm around Betty's shoulders.

That, as any member of the OD Connected crew might profanely explain, was just about the most foolish action he could have chosen to make. Betty did not even think of using her derringer, for she knew of a better and less permanent way of discouraging the amorous cowhand. In addition to teaching Dusty the secrets of jujitsu and karate, her grandfather's Japanese servant had passed on the knowledge to Betty. She proved to be an apt pupil, as her actions showed.

Before the big blond girl could think of doing anything to help, Betty apparently yielded to the cowhand's attentions. Slipping her right arm around his waist, Betty walked on a couple of strides and altered her pace until in step with him. As the cowhand's right foot landed on the ground, Betty moved her own ahead and central to his legs. Bringing her left foot alongside the right, Betty bent her knees slightly, rammed her buttocks against him, and thrust back hard. At the same moment she twisted her body to the left and forced forward with the encircling arm. Much to Ilsa's—and the cowhand's—amazement, he sailed over to light down on his back with a thud that jarred the wind from his body.

Although ready to continue her defense to even more painful limits, Betty decided such would not be necessary. Taken by surprise, the cowhand just lay sprawled on the ground.

"When you stop seeing all the pretty lights, I should go down to the Bon Ton dance hall, cowboy," Betty remarked. "Come on, Ilsa."

"I saw it, but I don't believe it!" Ilsa gasped. "How'd you do it?"

"My grandfather's servant taught me. Only I'm a beginner compared to some of the things Tommy Okasi can do."

Telling a mildly incredulous Ilsa about some of the *tameshiwari* feats, breaking wood with the bare hands or feet, that she had seen Tommy Okasi perform, Betty strolled on in the direction of the Bull's Head saloon. Laughter, shouts, and loud singing came to their ears as they approached the rear of the building. Even without Ilsa's information, Betty would have known that **they** had reached their destination. From inside the building came the words of the old Confederate anthem, not the mild lyrics written by its composer, Daniel D. Emmett, but the militantly patriotic words of General Albert Pike, CSA.

> Southrons, hear your country call you!
> Up lest worse than death befall you!
> To arms, to arms, to arms, in Dixie!
> Advance the flag of Dixie!
> Hurrah! Hurrah!
> For Dixie-land we take our stand,
> And live or die for Dixie.
> To arms! To arms! We'll fight them all for Dixie.
> To arms! To arms! We'll fight the world for Dixie.

"If music be the food of love, that bunch in there're sure starved for affection," Betty said, but her eyes were bright as she remembered hearing the same song roared out by the Texas Light Cavalry while her grandfather's men held Arkansas south of the Ouachita River against the outnumbering Yankee army. "Now here's a piece of luck."

The latter comment came as Billy Jack emerged from the saloon's rear entrance and stood looking around in a cautious manner that·intrigued Betty. More so as, when he saw the two girls, he immediately assumed an innocent air.

"Why, howdy, Miss Betty," he greeted her in just too casual a tone. A glint of approval came into his eyes as he studied Ilsa and continued, "Howdy, ma'am. Nice night if it don't blow up a storm."

"Hold hard there!" Betty snapped as Billy Jack turned toward the door.

"You wanting something, Miss Betty?" he inquired mildly, yet giving the impression that he intended to bolt at any moment.

"I want to see Dusty and Red. Can you fetch them for me?"

"Well, I'd say yes to that, I reckon. You wanting to see them real particular now?"

"*Real* particular," said Betty, the guileless behavior not fooling her in the least. "What's happened, Billy Jack?"

"Happened?" he repeated. "I'll go fetch them for you."

"Hold hard there!" Betty snapped as he swung away and dived for the door.

"Yes, ma'am," Billy Jack called back over his shoulder. "I'll sure tell 'em that you're here."

"Come back here, you long-legged, narrow-ribbed, scrawny-necked calamity wailer!" Betty yelled, but Billy Jack disappeared through the door like a redheaded woodpecker diving into its nest.

Letting out a frustrated snort, Betty watched the door close and realized that Billy Jack had taken refuge in one of the few places that a strong-willed young lady of good breeding could not follow. So she could do nothing but wait, fuming and seething with curiosity, until her cousins chose to appear. That did not take long, and Betty noticed how both of them eyed her apprehensively.

"Why, howdy, Cousin Betty," Dusty greeted her.

"This sure is a pleasant surprise," Red continued, with all the forced joviality of a politician who had been wet on while kissing a baby.

"All right," Betty said through gritted teeth. "What's happened?"

"Would you believe me if I said nothing?" asked Dusty.

"I doubt it. Anyways, I've not come to bring your sins down on your fool heads. I want you to do something for me."

"Such as?" asked Red cautiously.

"It's important," the girl assured them.

Instantly Dusty and Red became serious. The expression on their cousin's face warned them that something more than a mere inquiry about their reason for being involved in a shooting lay behind Betty's arrival.

"What's up, Betty?" Dusty asked.

Quickly the girl told of the incident at the Maybelle house and could have quite cheerfully strangled Ilsa, who insisted on going into details of the snake's eviction. While Betty expected her cousins to be interested, she found their startled exchange of glances hard to understand.

"Let's go talk to Miss Maybelle," Dusty said quietly, cutting into Ilsa's story.

"It'd be best," Red said. "First me, now this."

"You?" Betty put in.

"Two jaspers tried to bushwhack me when I walked out of the front a piece back," Red explained. "I had to shoot one of 'em."

"So that's why Billy Jack—"

"Sure, Betty," Dusty replied. "We've had some of the boys come out and make sure there were no more of them around."

"I meant why he acted like he'd a burr in his pants' seat," Betty said. "But why would anybody want to shoot you, Cousin Red?"

"That's a good question," Dusty admitted, "trouble being we can't think up an answer."

"The two incidents can't be connected," Betty stated. "Red's hardly met Sarah Maybelle."

"Could be somebody was after you, not her," Dusty pointed out. "Anybody who knows you would guess that you'd be fool enough to try some crazy game."

"Why, thank you, Cousin Dusty." Betty smiled. "Are you coming?"

"Right now. Just let Red go tell the boys that we've been called away for a spell and we'll go with you."

Having stepped into the saloon, Red passed the message on and assured the gathered company that its services would not be needed. On rejoining his cousins and Ilsa, he overheard something that started a train of thought going.

"Does Miss Maybelle have any idea who might have sent that snake?" Dusty was asking when Red returned.

"She thinks it's a boy who used to court her before she met Sandy," Betty answered. "It was his handwriting on the note with the basket. Only that, being so, spoils our theory of a foul plot to wipe out the pride of the Hardin, Fog, and Blaze clan. Doesn't it?"

"It sure does," Dusty agreed.

"Hey, though," Red said, "I've just had a thought—"

"I knew he'd have to start one day," Betty interrupted. "Of course, it's being married to a real smart lil girl that brought it on."

"Make like she's not here, Cousin Red," suggested Dusty.

"I've been trying to do *that* for years. Anyways, Dusty, I just remembered that I let Sandy try on my vest soon after we started the fun. If that jasper I shot'd been asking Stormy about us right then, he'd have seen Sandy wearing it—"

"And when you came out of the saloon with it on, he and his pard made a mistake," Dusty finished for Red. "They were after Sandy McGraw, not you."

4

Red's news threw an entirely different light on the affair and helped explain away one of the puzzling aspects, the motive for the attempted killing. Where there did not appear to be a reason for anybody to want Red dead, a very good one applied to Sandy McGraw: a jealous young man trying to take revenge on the girl who rejected him and the man of her choice.

"Was the man you shot a young German?" Betty asked Red, and did not wait for an answer. "No, he couldn't have been or somebody would've recognized him."

"He was just a cheap hired gun," Dusty told her. "Do you know this jasper we're talking about, Miss Swenson?"

During the time the others had been talking, Ilsa stood silent, although an interested listener. She also stared wonderingly at Dusty, finding it hard to reconcile the small, insignificant-appearing young man with his almost legendary fame. All through the war Captain Dusty Fog ranked high among Dixie's fighting heroes, and in Texas his fame exceeded that of the

South's other two leading cavalry raiders, John Singleton Mosby or Turner Ashby. Slowly the force of Dusty's personality grew until Ilsa no longer thought of him in mere size but felt he stood the tallest person present.

"You mean Chester Finwald? Yes, I know him. His father sent him East to college, and he started courting Sarah when he came back. Only she always preferred Sandy. So would I."

"How'd Finwald take it when he heard that Sarah was going to marry Sandy?"

"He didn't like it, Captain Fog, that's for sure."

"Would he have any money?" Red inquired.

"Well, he works in his father's store and never seems short," Ilsa replied.

"That jasper you shot wouldn't be a hundred-a-month-and-found man, Red," Dusty pointed out. "You wouldn't know where I can find Finwald, Miss Swenson?"

"You might try the Casa Moreno Hotel's bar," the girl replied. "I heard Papa saying he'd seen Chester and the Soehnen brothers there quite often lately."

"We'll see you ladies home and then try there," Dusty decided. "What'd you tell the boys, Red?"

"That Cousin Betty said we'd got to go with her. That way they all knew we'd no choice but do it."

"What a sweet child," Betty purred. "Anyways, Sue gave me orders to make sure you behaved while we're here, Cousin Red."

"Women!" Red snorted.

"Men!" Betty countered.

While talking, the party had begun to walk in the direction of the Maybelle house. Before they covered much of the distance, Betty saw the drunken young cowhand approaching. Coming to a halt, he stared at the girls and backed away.

"Hey, fellers," he called, "come here!"

"What's up, friend?" Dusty asked with a grin.

"It's a secret."

Alert for a possible trick, Dusty and Red left the girls and walked over to the cowhand. Gravely he pointed in Betty's direction and dropped his voice to a confidential whisper.

"You wan' watch that there lil gal. She's mean as hell. You just say one wrong word, and she'll throw you clear over her head one-handed. Left-handed at that."

Having done what he regarded as his duty to his fellowmen by giving the warning, the cowhand turned and ambled off as fast as his legs would carry him. Betty watched him go and studied the grins on her cousins'· faces. While not sure what caused the cowhand's warning, Dusty and Red could imagine how Betty had created such an impression on him.

"What did he want?" she asked.

"Just told us something we already knew," Red answered. "Let's go."

With which Betty had to be satisfied, for neither of her cousins offered any further enlightenment. Before she could enforce her demands for information, they reached their destination and put aside levity. Taking Sarah aside in the sitting room, Dusty questioned her thoroughly and felt sure that she told the truth. Although certain Finwald wrote the note, Sarah insisted that he only intended the snake as a joke and felt sure he would not hire a killer as a means of disposing of his rival. Dusty did not feel so sure and decided to interview Finwald at the earliest possible moment.

Having left the girls without announcing his intentions, Dusty went with Red to the Casa Moreno Hotel. Business had not improved in the bar, and only Finwald's party stood at the counter when the two cousins entered. Murphy had returned earlier and, to establish an alibi, joked with the bartender about needing a good dose of croton oil to make his trips out back of a shorter duration. When satisfied that the other felt sure he had never left the hotel, Murphy had bought a drink apiece, asked about the forthcoming snake- and cockfights, and then left.

Concern flickered across Finwald's face as he saw Dusty and Red enter. Then he took in Dusty's small size and established to his satisfaction that both the Soehnen brothers outweighed Red, so felt more at ease.

"Is your name Finwald?" Dusty asked, halting behind the young man.

"So what if it is?" Finwald snorted, not turning to face the speaker.

"So if it is, I'd like to see you outside."

"What about?"

"Your choice in wedding gifts."

"Did McGraw send you?" Finwald snarled, still not turning, although his companions moved away from him and halted, standing beyond the two cousins.

"Sandy doesn't know about it yet," Dusty replied. "That's why I've come. If he finds out, it's likely to be more than a licking he gives you."

Studying the insignificant-appearing shape reflected in the bar's mirror, Finwald transferred some of his hatred of Sandy in Dusty's direction. Finwald had all the egotistical, self-opinionated, arrogant superiority a college education gives to a certain mentality and so objected to such a runty nobody's addressing him like that. Without the Soehnen brothers' presence, Finwald would have controlled his emotions or taken them out on something even less dangerous-looking than the small cowhand. Given their backing, the advantage of numbers and heft, he felt that he might safely make his play, provided he used his brilliant mentality to outwit the two cowboys.

"All right," he said, smiling disarmingly and starting to turn. "We'll go outside and talk."

And saying it, he launched a punch at Dusty's head. It was, in Finwald's considered opinion, a fast, powerful, well-delivered blow guaranteed to take the small man by surprise. Unfortunately Dusty did not regard it in that light. To a man of Dusty's considerable *practical* experience, every move Finwald made was telegraphed as if the other had shouted his intentions at the top of his voice.

Before Finwald completed the turn, Dusty measured the distance with his eye. As the other struck, the small man stepped aside and at the same time thrust at Finwald's outdriving right arm. Cupping his hand slightly, Dusty deflected the arm downward and aside in such a manner that it turned Finwald's whole body slightly away from him. Finwald was caught unawares, and his momentum carried him forward and past

Dusty. Pivoting around, Dusty drew his right arm up, bent it across his chest, and then lashed it out. He struck in the *tegatana,* hand sword, of karate: fingers extended and together, thumb bent across his palm. The heel of Dusty's hand chopped at the back of Finwald's head, missing the base of the skull, and sent the young townsman stumbling across the room.

In dealing with Finwald, Dusty turned his back on Fritz Soehnen. Never one to pass up an opportunity, Fritz lunged forward with big hands reaching out. Dusty had not been entirely unaware of the danger and kept on the alert for it. Plain to his ears came the thud of Fritz's feet, and he spun smoothly around to face the brawny youngster.

Bringing up both hands, Dusty blocked Fritz's reaching arms from the inside and forced them apart. From there, before Fritz could close his grip once more, Dusty's hands curled in to clamp hold of the other's lapels. Already Fritz's momentum carried him forward. He saw Dusty seem to disappear; then a foot rammed into his midsection, and he felt himself first falling forward, then sailing up and over to land with a crash on his back.

When Finwald swung on Dusty, Hans Soehnen leaped at Red. Around San Antonio Soehnen had built up a name as a fighter. However, the reputation had been gained against other town dwellers or young cowhands from the local ranches. Such opponents lacked skill, and Soehnen's brawn brought him victory. That did not apply to Red. Trained well and brought up in a hard school, Red fought with his head instead of relying on plain muscle. Slipping the slow, if power-packed, punch Soehnen threw at him, Red ripped a left into the German's belly. With a grunt, Soehnen halted in his tracks. On the heels of the left, Red's right hand drove up under the German's jaw and snapped his head back. Across whipped the left, which collided with Soehnen's cheek and tumbled him into the bar. For all that, when Red came in, the German slashed a backhand blow home. Red staggered, caught his balance, and met the other's rush with a brace of hard, accurate fists.

Hitting a table halted Finwald's staggering form. For a moment he clung to it and then turned in time to see Dusty flip

Fritz Soehnen with a *tomoe-nage* stomach throw. One glance told Finwald that he could expect no help from the elder brother. However, he decided there might be a chance to fix his small assailant, provided that he moved quickly enough. So he thrust himself away from the table, charged across the room, and launched a kick in Dusty's direction.

Already in the process of rising, Dusty saw the foot coming at him. His left hand shot out under the leg and heaved upward. Then he completed getting to his feet and with a twisting heave tumbled Finwald into the bar. Before Dusty could follow Finwald up, he saw Fritz rising. While breathing hard and shaken by the throw, the young German still presented a danger that Dusty knew could not be overlooked—especially when Fritz caught up a chair and rushed forward, swinging it into the air.

Before Fritz came close enough to make use of the fairly lethal weapon, Dusty went into a rolling dive that carried him under its arc of swing. The small Texan's left shoulder formed the roller on which his body turned, and in what appeared to be one continuous motion he regained his feet. Linking his fingers, Dusty smashed both hands onto the back of Fritz's neck, and the youngster shot forward. The chair had struck the floor when it missed its original objective, and the force of Dusty's blow drove Fritz onto its back. Wood splintered, and Fritz pitched over the chair to land sprawled out on the floor.

From the corner of his eye Dusty saw Finwald rushing at him again and prepared to deal with the attack. The abortive earlier attempts had given Finwald caution, and he skidded to a halt before coming too close. By that time Dusty had grown angry enough to decide on his next course of action. Leaping forward, he shot out his right hand to clamp hold thumb downward of Finwald's right bicep. At the same time Dusty's left hand thrust the trapped forearm back as the small Texan began to pass Finwald. Pivoted around so that he stood behind the young man, Dusty entwined his left arm under, then over Finwald's trapped right and levered up at it. A yell of pain broke from Finwald, increasing to a screech as the steel-tough fingers of Dusty's right hand clamped hold of the back of his neck. Dusty did not grip centrally, but to the left so that his thumb gouged into the mastoid area.

Throughout the fight so far the bartender continued to lean on the counter and watch. Apart from one chair there had been no damage to the house's property, and a fight relieved the boredom on such a dull night. While he found Red and Hans Soehnen's part in the affair interesting, it lacked the novel aspects shown in Dusty's handling of two larger men.

Then the bartender saw something that caused him to intervene. Muttering bilingual curses, Fritz Soehnen rose from the shattered chair. The young German dipped a hand into his pocket and drew a folding dirk knife, opening its six-inch-long blade.

"Put it away, Soehnen!" yelled the bartender.

A fistfight was one thing, but the introduction of the knife brought too serious an aspect into the affair for the bartender to remain silent.

Hearing the words, Dusty concluded that his German opponent must be bringing some weapon or other into use. It could not be the other Soehnen doing so, for he stood to one side, both big hands clamped on Red's throat. Dusty knew better than to wait for further proof. Freeing Finwald's arm, he hurled the young man away from him and turned fast in Fritz's direction.

Even before he saw the knife, Dusty started his right hand flashing across to the butt of the left-side Colt and went into the stance rapidly becoming known as the gunfighter's crouch. Legs apart and slightly bent, body inclined forward, the Colt finishing as the central point of his entire being, Dusty threw down on Fritz Soehnen. That knife the German held was not the kind of thing made to be carried in the pocket and put to general use, but a deadly weapon. No less so because its wielder could not be termed a master knifefighter. Certainly Dusty did not intend to take chances.

"Drop it!" the small Texan barked, backing his words with the cocked and lined long-barreled Army Colt.

Stopping dead in his tracks, Soehnen stared with an open mouth, and his suddenly limp fingers opened to let the knife clatter to the floor. He could hardly believe his eyes, yet the small cowhand undoubtedly held a Colt in what, a bare three-quarters of a second before, had been an empty hand. And suddenly the cowhand was small no more. In some manner he appeared to have taken on size until he dominated the room, exuding a deadly menace that went beyond a mere cocked revolver.

Satisfied that he did not need to worry further about Fritz for the moment, Dusty darted a glance in Red's direction. It rapidly became apparent that Red needed no help in dealing with the second Soehnen. Clasping his hands together without interlacing the fingers, Red prepared to free himself from the powerful grip on his throat. Out lashed the redhead's left foot, catching Hans Soehnen hard on the shin and drawing a yelp of pain. Driving his hands up, Red forced apart Hans's arms but did not break the hold. So Red continued to raise his hands between Hans's arms and then brought them down. The two hands thudded solidly onto the bridge of Hans's nose, and pain caused him to relax his hold. Pulling himself free from the German's hands, Red glided in a pace, and his clenched left fist sank almost wrist-deep into Hans's belly. With a croaking gasp that expelled most of the air from his lungs, Hans doubled over. His face came down just right to meet Red's other hand, which worked in concert with the left. A solid click sounded, and Hans straightened out, struck the bar, bounced off to catch Red's left fist solidly at the side of the jaw. Spinning around, Hans toppled to the floor, sighed once, and went limp.

With Hans disposed of without the kind of fight Red had hoped to enjoy, the redhead turned to see if he could be of any assistance to his illustrious cousin. While Dusty clearly needed none with the younger Soehnen, Finwald appeared to be taking advantage of the small Texan's preoccupation. Being behind Dusty, the slim trouble causer reached for the bottle from which he and his companions had shared drinks earlier. Cold anger glinted in Red's eyes as he lunged by his cousin, clamped a hold on Finwald's shoulder, turned, and hit him. Finwald shot away from the bottle and landed in a sitting position on the floor. But not for long. Following him up, Red took hold of his lapels and hauled him erect.

"Don't fuss me anymore, boy!" Red warned, slamming Finwald back against the bar. "My favorite lil cousin was in that room when Sarah Maybelle opened your present."

"Ho-horned lizards are harmless!" Finwald squawked.

That was the truth. *Phrynosoma cornutum,* known as a horned toad to most folks west of the Mississippi but, as Finwald correctly claimed, a lizard, might look revoltingly dangerous and be thought poisonous. It was not, being a harmless creature whose sole means of defense consisted of squirting drops of blood from the forward corners of the eyes.

"Horned lizards might be!" Red conceded. "But that damned rattlesnake sure as hell wasn't."

No amount of college-educated superiority could give Finwald an argument to that statement. From the earliest days of its life, a rattlesnake carried sufficient venom in its poison sacs to be deadly dangerous. Popular belief even claimed that a rattlesnake killed at any time during the day could still strike and eject its venom until sundown. However, Finwald did not seem to know what Red meant.

"Ra-rattlesnake!" he yelped. "What rattlesnake?"

"The one in that basket!" Red growled, drawing Finwald forward and backing him hard into the counter again. Releasing his hold with one hand, Red knotted it into a useful-looking fist. "I've a mind to—"

"Don't hit me!" Finwald screeched. "My father'll have the law on you!"

"Ease off, Red," Dusty ordered, for the threat did not seem to be working. Holstering his Colt, he looked at Fritz. "Go tend to your brother."

Without a word and leaving his knife where it lay, Fritz obeyed. Then Dusty turned his attention to the cowering Finwald, who, on being released by Red, cringed against the bar.

"It was only a joke!" Finwald blubbered.

"You call sending a rattlesnake in a basket to a roomful of girls a joke?" Dusty demanded.

"I suppose sending those two jaspers to gun Sandy McGraw down was to keep you laughing for a week," Red went on.

"I—I don't know what you mean!" Finwald croaked, trying to sink into himself before the two pairs of coldly menacing eyes that bored into him.

All former traces of Finwald's self-opinionated superiority had left him, and he could think of nothing coherent to say. No flow of wit to blast the two Texans into a sense of their inferior educational status left Finwald. Instead he just hung on the bar and muttered weakly.

After rising from his brother's side, Fritz Soehnen approached Dusty. The young German had heard enough to tell him that something had gone wrong with their stupid and thoughtless joke, something serious that could bring back repercussions on those involved. While Finwald's father might be 'progressive' and overlook his son's bad behavior, the same did not apply to Papa Soehnen. There would be trouble enough when Soehnen senior heard his sons had been involved in a saloon brawl, and the small Texan hinted at something even more serious.

"Hans and me don't know anything about Chester and Sandy McGraw, mister," Fritz stated. "But I do know there was only horned toads in the basket."

"You're sure, huh?" Dusty said quietly.

"Hans and me helped Chester catch them."

"And the basket never went out of your sight?"

"No."

"There was only a bunch of horned toads in it, Cap'n Fog," the bartender said. "I saw 'em when they opened the basket one time."

Probably for the first time in his life Chester Finwald felt gratitude to another person. At that moment he could have fallen on Fritz Soehnen's bull neck with cries of joy and repeated it on the bartender. Then he realized that the two cowhands would be a whole lot harder to convince than his doting father, who always treated complaints leveled against Chester as the bigoted persecution of opposing political views.

"I couldn't've carried a live rattlesnake under my jacket,"

Finwald began with just a touch of his old superiority. It died away again as Dusty swung to face him.

"Maybe you saw one on your way to the Maybelle place and decided to change your wedding gift," Dusty suggested.

"He couldn't have, Cap—" Fritz began, then realized the meaning of the name he started to repeat. His eyes bugged out, and he stared at the small Texan. "Did he say Cap'n Fog?"

"That's right, Fritz boy," the bartender told him with relish. "You tried to pull a knife on Cap'n Dusty Fog."

Earlier that evening Fritz might have scoffed at the idea of such a small, insignificant young man being the almost legendary Dusty Fog. That would have been *before* he felt the strength in the small man's hands, learned the other's skill at bare-handed fighting, or witnessed the lightning speed with which the Colt came into Dusty's hand.

"I—I'm sorry, Cap'n," he apologized.

"So all you took was a basket of horned toads?" Dusty asked.

"Yes, that's all!" whined Finwald.

"It's the cross-my-heart-and-hope-to-die truth, Cap'n," confirmed Fritz.

"Could anybody have changed the baskets without your knowing?"

"Not unless they did it after Chester left it on the Maybelles' porch."

"Who else'd know about this fool game of yours?" Red demanded.

"Nobody," admitted Fritz, looking deflated.

"One feller would," the bartender put in. "He heard you talking right here."

"Who was he?" asked Dusty.

"A medium-sized hardcase, looked like a half-breed and a hired gun."

5

When giving the brief description, the bartender did not expect it to arouse such interest from his illustrious guests. Dusty and Red exchanged glances and then directed a long, searching stare at Finwald.

"How was this feller dressed?" asked Red of the bartender.

"Sombrero, charro jacket, string tie. Got him a low-tied gun."

"A Colt?" Dusty inquired.

"Naw. The butt wasn't right."

Few contemporary revolvers carried butts with the smooth, hand-fitting shape of those produced by the Colt company. Already the products of Colonel Sam Colt's Hartford factory had achieved such ubiquity throughout the West that any other type of revolver tended to catch the eye. While the bartender failed to recognize Murphy's Allen & Wheelock revolver as such, he noticed it was not a Colt. The same fact struck Stormy

Weather, to be mentioned in his description of the second of
Red's assailants.

"Where is he now?" growled Red.

"Dunno," admitted the bartender. "He came in while this
bunch were talking. I thought he'd come for the snakefights
and told him he was a day early."

"Snakefights?"

"Sure, Cap'n Fog. We hold 'em in the cellar every once in a
while. When we can get enough snakes."

"You've enough now?"

"Maybe a dozen rattlers and the same number of kings down
there right now."

Once more Dusty and Red exchanged glances. Then the
small Texan resumed his questioning. "What did this hardcase
do?"

"Had a drink and allowed to be going out back. He didn't
come back for a longish time, set up another drink or so, then
left."

"He went out just before we left to deliver the present," Fritz
added, and darted to his brother's side as Hans showed signs of
recovery. Dropping to one knee, he blurted a rapid mouthful of
German at Hans, of which only the words *Kapitän Fog*
sounded familiar to the listeners. Clearly Fritz gave warning of
Dusty's identity and explained the situation, for although he
looked sullen and glared at Red, Hans offered to cause no trouble when he rose.

"He sure did," said the bartender as Hans lurched to and
leaned against the counter. "Fact being he only come back after
this bunch. I mentioned it'd taken him some time, and he said
he'd have to take croton oil."

"How many snakes have you down in the cellar?" asked
Dusty.

"Couldn't say for sure, Cap'n," the bartender replied. "The
boss'd know."

"How's he keep them?"

"In baskets—say, they're just like the one Finwald had."

"So they should be," Finwald put in. "They come from my
father's store."

"Go ask your boss if he'll count his snakes, friend," Dusty requested.

Normally the owner of the hotel would have objected to being disturbed or maybe refused to comply with the request for information. Knowing this, the bartender made sure his employer knew the identity of the man requiring the assistance. Within five minutes of hearing that Captain Dusty Fog required his services, the hotel's owner stood in the bar and said that one of his snakes was missing.

"I don't know anything about it!" Finwald wailed.

Watching the Germans, Dusty concluded that they at least had no knowledge of any murderous intentions Finwald may have had. While Finwald's protestations of innocence appeared genuine enough, Dusty wanted to make certain before accepting them.

"Maybe you don't," Dusty said. "But was I you, I'd hunt a hole and hide in it until after the wedding's over and Sandy McGraw's headed for San Garcia."

"You do that," Red said. "Happen Sandy hears about the fool game you pulled, he'll beat your brains back in."

Leaving the hotel, Dusty and Red made their way to the marshal's office and arrived in time to find Dale just finishing tossing a drunken cowhand into one of the cells. On hearing of the incident at the Maybelle house, Dale replied that already a woman in the neighborhood had arrived with a complaint that somebody had thrown a basket containing half a dozen horned lizards into her front garden.

"That clears Finwald," remarked Red, always willing to see good in everybody.

"Or shows that he's playing tricky," Dusty answered. "He could have hired those two jaspers who tried to kill you and rigged the whole game."

"Look, Dusty," Dale said, "I don't like the Finwalds, father or son, but I don't think Chester'd pull a game like that. A meanness like trying to spoil Sarah's bridal shower with the horned toads, sure, but not a killing, even by hiring it done."

"A man in love does mighty foolish and unusual things, so I've heard," Dusty replied.

"All Chester Finwald ever loved was hisself." Dale snorted. "Sure it hurt his pride when Sarah picked a better man, but not enough for him to pay out good money hiring killers."

"I can't think of anybody else who'd want Sandy dead," Dusty objected.

"Sandy never owned a ranch before either," Red pointed out.

"There's that," Dusty admitted. "Where'd be the most likely place for a half-breed hardcase to stay around town, Anse?"

"Rosa Rio's cantina," Dale replied.

"Then let's go pay her a visit," the small Texan suggested.

Built on the edge of the Mexican quarter of San Antonio, Rosa Rio's adobe cantina served as a kind of international melting pot. While she drew some trade from both Americans and Mexicans, the bulk of her customers consisted of men of mixed racial blood. Unlike the Casa Moreno, the cantina had a good crowd inside. However, when Dale, Dusty, and Red entered, the noise died away. Hard faces with cold, unfriendly eyes studied the trio suspiciously or darted glances at the other exits from the room.

"I've seen rattlesnakes that looked friendlier," Red commented quietly.

"Rattlers're nothing compared with some of this bunch," Dale informed him. "And Rosa Rio behind the bar there's the worst of them all."

From her usual place at the cash drawer behind the counter, Rosa Rio flashed Dale a gold-toothed smile that had no mirth and did not reach her eyes. In her youth she might have been voluptuous, but little of it remained. Drink and general dissipation had left her bloatedly fat and wiped all but the last traces of what had been a great beauty from her face.

"*Buenos noches,* Marshal," she said. "You want a drink?"

"I thought we were friends, Rosa," Dale replied.

"Oh, it won't be the stuff I sell," the woman assured him, darting a glance in Dusty's direction. "What else can I do for you?"

"We're looking for a man—"

"I run a clean, respectable place here!" Rosa squawked.

"Why, sure," said Dale, sounding almost as if he believed

her. "He's a half-breed, Rosa. Stocky, middle-tall, wears a sombrero, charro jacket, white shirt, and string tie. Got a low-tied gun and a knife stuck down his boot."

"I've got a roomful like that." The woman giggled. "Most of my customers dress border style."

"We'll take a look around then," Dale stated.

"Feel free. You got new deputies?"

"You might say that."

"San Antonio must be getting rich." Rosa grinned.

"How's that?" Dale asked.

"Taking on Dusty Fog and Red Blaze as deputy marshals," the woman explained. "Go anyplace you like and see what you want."

Turning from the bar, Dusty looked around the room. Despite Rosa's claims, only three of her customers really fitted the somewhat scanty description on which Dusty's party worked. While the majority of the bar's occupants dressed in the fashion of Rio Grande dwellers, the trio alone possessed the necessary physical qualifications. One of them had a scar on his face that could not be missed, and that eliminated him. Such an identifying mark would have been noticed by either Stormy Weather or the Casa Moreno bartender and been mentioned when giving his description.

So Dusty started forward in the direction of the nearest suspect. To reach him, Dusty's party had to pass probably the only two men in the room who did not interest the small Texan. Tall, lean, obviously *americanos del norte,* the pair wore clothing of the kind rarely seen in southern Texas, hailing as it did from north country ranges. Unless Dusty missed his guess, the pair spent most of the time in the Dakotas or maybe even Wyoming. They certainly would never have caused the experienced Stormy Weather to mistake them, either of them, for a half-breed of the Rio Grande border country.

Suddenly the two men moved. Coming to his feet, the taller of the pair grabbed at his holstered Colt. No less swiftly the second man sent his chair flying backward and fanged a hand toward the gun on his hip. They moved fast and might have taken the advancing trio by complete surprise except for one small but vitally important detail.

Being trained and experienced peace officers, Dusty and Dale approached the man they meant to question in the correct manner, ready to handle any violent objections he offered to them. So the first hostile move, even though it came from an unexpected area, triggered off an instant response.

Dusty's hands crossed in a flickering move so fast the eye could barely follow it. Steel rasped on leather as the bone-handled Colts came clear, their barrels turned outward and lined on the two men. Flame lashed from each of Dusty's Colts, and the crash of both charges of exploding black powder sounded so close together that they came as one single sound. For all that, the man at the right spun around to fall with a bullet between his eyes, and the second took lead in his chest. Reeling backward, the second man caught his legs against the thrown-over chair and went down with his revolver dropping from his hand. So fast had Dusty moved that while their guns cleared leather, neither man found time to shoot.

On the heels of Dusty's shots, Dale and Red brought out their guns and saw they would not need to shoot. Instead they prepared to handle any trouble made by members of the crowd. Crashes sounded as the side doors of the room burst open and Dale's deputies came in, holding shotguns. Knowing the nature of Rosa Rio's usual class of clientele, Dale had taken no chances and had brought reinforcements along.

"Stay put!" Red ordered the man Dusty wished to question and halted his attempt to rise. Sinking back into his chair, the man glared at Dusty's party but made no hostile moves.

Stepping forward, Dale looked at the two shot men. Recognizing neither of them, he turned toward the bar.

"Rosa!" he barked. "Come here!"

Slowly, reluctantly, it seemed, the woman ambled around the counter and across the room. "Yes?" she asked sullenly.

"Who are they?"

"How would I know?"

"Because you're a nosy old bitch who makes it her business to know things," Dale answered. "I'd bet you know every man in this room's name, history, and damned near down to the last nickel in his pocket."

If the woman felt any pleasure at the tribute to her knowledge, she hid it. Nor did she offer to make any answer to the question. Holstering his Colts, Dusty turned to his cousin.

"Go get the boys down here from the Bull's Head, Cousin Red," he said.

Instead of being pleased by the prospect of a further thirty or more potential customers, Rosa looked disconcerted. Little happened in or around San Antonio that she did not learn about sooner or later, and she was well aware of what brought Dusty to the city. All too well she knew that the ex-members of Company C would follow any order their leader gave. If Dusty told them to do so, they would wreck her place. Rosa decided that she was in no position to resist the marshal's request for information.

"They're Camella Hanks and Peep O'Day, from the Hole-in-the-Wall bunch."

"And why're they here?" Dale growled, for that particular gang did not operate in Texas.

"I don't know. They came in and asked for Starke Reynolds."

"He's one of the Kimble County gang," Dusty commented.

"I've heard of him," Dale replied. "Now what the hell would he be wanting with a couple of north country yahoos?"

"One thing's for sure," Rosa remarked, not without a hint of relief, as she looked at the two shapes on the floor. "They'll never tell you now."

Although the possibility of a meeting between representatives of two major outlaw gangs interested Dale, Dusty had other problems on his mind. So he stepped by the bodies and walked over to the man Red covered.

"Stand up, mister," the small Texan ordered.

"No knife and a Colt," Red said as the man obeyed. "It's not him."

"Most likely not," Dusty answered. "Where've you been all night?"

"Right here. Ask Rosa."

"Sure he has," the woman confirmed.

Nor did the second man carry the necessary armament, having no knife and sporting a brace of Navy Colts. However Dale instructed two of his deputies to take the men to his office, where the witnesses could see them and either confirm or deny their innocence.

"Who wants Sandy McGraw dead, Rosa?" Dusty asked as the men left.

"Does anybody?" she countered. "If so, I've not heard about it."

"But you'd hear if there was," Dusty insisted.

"Me, Cap'n?"

"Don't fuss me, Rosa!" Dusty warned. "I'm tired and riled that I'm missing a real pleasant evening with some old friends. Unless I get some straight answers, I'll fetch those same friends down here and tell them *you* helped with the hiring."

Sucking in a deep breath, the woman avoided meeting Dusty's cold eyes for a moment. When she raised her face to his, a hint of concern showed on the bloated features. While Anse Dale was an honest lawman devoted to maintaining the peace, he might possibly turn his back during the wrecking of *her* place. Only lack of evidence enabled Rosa to continue in business, although the marshal suspected the truth, that she had a finger in most of the criminal activities around San Antonio. So Dale just might take advantage of Dusty's anger to rid himself of a problem.

"If I knew who you wanted, I'd be able to help better," she said sullenly.

"We told you," Dusty pointed out.

"Can you tell me more about him?"

"I don't know much more," Dusty admitted frankly. "Like we said, medium-sized, stocky, looks part Irish. The gun he wears isn't a Colt, although I don't know what it might be, and he totes a knife in a boot sheath."

"That sounds like Paco Murphy," the woman said thoughtfully. "At least he doesn't use a Colt and carries an Arkansas toothpick in his boot top."

"Who is this Murphy?" demanded Red.

"A *pistolero valiente.* Well, maybe he's not so *valiente,* but there's worse around."

A *pistolero,* used in that manner, meant a hired gun; the *valiente* part indicated him to be a man of courage and ability above the average.

"Is he around San Antonio?" Dusty inquired, wondering if the woman was as worried by his threat as she appeared.

"If he is, I've not seen him," she replied, meeting Dusty's gaze without flinching. "He used to work up around El Paso mostly."

"Who'd he work with?"

"Nobody special. If he needed help, he'd hire it local and as cheap as he could manage. But like I said, I haven't seen Paco Murphy in months."

"Would you know if he was in town, Rosa?" Red drawled.

"Me! Why should I know about a man like that? I run an honest business, do no harm to anybody, treat folks fair—"

Looking at the woman, Dusty decided that he had never seen anybody but the Ysabel Kid manage such a piously innocent tone. Only the Kid never adopted that particular expression and voice unless wanting to hide some deed he found necessary but felt would not meet with Dusty's approval.

"You watch that shining halo doesn't slip down around your neck and choke you, Rosa," Dale interrupted. "Do you want to search the place, Dusty?"

"Sure!" Rosa yelled. "Search it. I insist you search it so that you know I don't hide this feller you want."

"Watch things down here, boys," the marshal ordered, and his deputies took a firmer hold on the shotguns that kept the crowd under control. "Let's go, Dusty, and you can come up with us, Rosa."

Muttering curses under her breath in complaint at the enforced exercise, Rosa followed Dale, Dusty, and Red up the stairs. There she knocked on the first door and yelled for the room's occupants to open up. Going from room to room, Dusty and the others checked on the occupants. They did not find the man but embarrassed a couple of otherwise respectable San Antonio citizens visiting ladies of doubtful virtue and were cursed by an all-but-naked girl alone in one room for disturbing her rest.

"Satisfied?" demanded Rosa, in the manner of a vindicated martyr, as they left the last room.

"If he'd been here, you wouldn't've let us search," Dale answered. "Have some of your *hombres* tote those two bodies down to the coroner's office, Rosa."

"Sure," she answered.

"And if Starke Reynolds comes to town, I want to know."

"You could get me killed, Marshal," the woman whined.

"I'm not that lucky," Dale assured her. "You'd live through two plagues and one massacre."

Directing a look of pure hatred at Dale, the old woman returned to the barroom and gave orders for the removal of the bodies. Then, as the lawmen followed the corpse-carrying party out, Rosa returned to behind the counter.

"What about it, Dusty?" Dale wanted to know.

"I don't know. Anse, that's for sure," Dusty replied. "He's not there, or he's mighty well hid. I'm going to see about guarding Sarah and Sandy."

"And I aim to go to the telegraph office," Dale stated. "I want to know why Hole-in-the-Wall and Kimble County owlhoots're meeting in my town."

Things quickly returned to normal in the cantina. Hostile visits by the law had never been so rare an occurrence in Rosa's place, and her clientele swiftly resumed their interrupted activities. After half an hour the two suspects returned, having been cleared by Stormy Weather and the Casa Moreno bartender. Giving orders to one of her hired hands, she waited until the man went outside and looked around. On being assured that no peace officers watched the building, Rosa left the counter and walked upstairs.

After knocking on the door of the lone girl's room, Rosa entered. She did not speak to the girl but addressed the large cupboard set into the wall. "You can come out now, Paco."

Slowly the door eased open, and Murphy emerged with his Allen & Wheelock held ready for use. Seeing that Rosa was alone, he grinned and holstered the gun.

"Thanks, Rosa," he said. "I was sure sweating in that cupboard."

"Then pay me and get the hell out of here," she answered.

"What's the rush?" he demanded. "I told you that I'm working in town."

"Sure. But you didn't tell me that you'd come to kill Dusty Fog's cousin."

"Who?"

"Red Blaze."

"But I'm after Sandy McGraw!" Murphy objected. "It was him I shot at outside the Bull's Head."

Shortly after Murphy's arrival and going upstairs to visit the girl, Rosa had learned details of the shooting. While not knowing how it came about, she guessed a mistake had been made.

"I don't know how you mistook Blaze for McGraw, him wearing that red and white calfskin vest," she said.

"Sure he was, when he came out of the Bull's Head," said Murphy. "That's how we knew it was McGraw. There wasn't another vest like it in the room."

"Only Red Blaze was wearing it," Rosa pointed out.

"Bl—But McGraw had it on in the saloon. Damned fool cow nurses. They must have changed vests after we left."

"It comes down to the same thing," Rosa stated. "You threw lead at Red Blaze no matter who you thought he was."

"So?" growled Murphy.

"I've always liked you, Paco, so I'm giving you a chance. Get the hell out of here pronto. I've done all I can to stop Fog from finding you. But I'm not chancing fuss with that Rio Hondo bunch, even without the other."

"What other?"

"The Hole-in-the-Wall bunch and Kimble County boys aren't going to like you when they hear what's happened."

"What has happened?" Murphy barked.

"Not much. Camella Hanks and Peep O'Day were killed downstairs. That was the shooting you sent Inez to look into."

"She told me two fellers'd been shot. What's it to do with me?"

"Dusty Fog came here looking for you. Camella and Peep thought the law was after them and went for their guns."

"That's all their misfortune," Murphy stated.

"And yours," Rosa replied. "They'd come down here to fix a big raid with the Kimble County boys. Now they're dead, and you're to blame for it."

A point Murphy had already grasped. Concern for his future welfare made him overlook an obvious point: how the two gangs would learn of his part in the affair. All too well he could imagine how the two gangs would react to the news that a two-bit hired gun had caused the deaths of Camella Hanks and Peep O'Day. They would not bother to think that Murphy had been merely a victim of circumstances, and their vengeance was likely to be painfully fatal.

Yet Murphy did not have the money for a protracted flight. Rosa's hospitality and assistance in avoiding the law did not come cheap. They ate deeply into the money advanced by his employer for killing McGraw and left little over. Of course, if he could complete his work, there would be a fair sum awaiting his collection. Not that he intended to let the woman know his plans.

"I'd best get the hell out of here," he told her. "I reckon I'll cut across to the east and lay low around Brownsville for a spell."

"It'd be best," the woman said.

Rosa always believed in playing every side of her hand. While she told Murphy's name to Dusty Fog, she did not betray the man's presence and so kept both parties fairly satisfied. After Murphy left the cantina, she sent one of her most trusted men off with word of Camella Hanks and Peep O'Day's death. In that way she guarded against the wrath to come, for she included details of Murphy's part in the affair as a means of exculpating herself.

6

Despite the hectic night before it, Sandy and Sarah's wedding passed off without a hitch. Certain of the bridegroom's friends appeared to be slightly the worse for wear as a result of the rowdiest and best bachelor party San Antonio could remember. However, the somewhat stiff carriage of Red Blaze, Billy Jack, and Stormy Weather came less from hangover than the fact that each of them carried an Army Colt concealed under his jacket. Nor did Dusty rely solely upon protecting the couple from within the church. Kiowa and a few others, who felt that the interior of church would hardly be the place for them, ringed the building, ready to prevent a murderous attempt on the outside.

So effective a screen did Dusty throw around the church and Sarah's home that Murphy saw no way he might carry out his work in safety. After a night spent sage-henning on the range, with the ground for a mattress and the sky his roof, the killer returned to San Antonio a changed man. Discarding most of the clothing he wore the previous night, he rode into town clad in a open-necked tartan shirt, bandanna, and Levi's pants, also altering the shape of his sombrero's crown to heighten the disguise. For all that, he retained his Allen & Wheelock revolver and boot knife. Although he carried a change of clothing in his war bag, he did not own spare weapons. In Texas at that time an unarmed man was more likely to attract attention than one who wore a gun, so he gambled on nobody's noticing the revolver.

Failing to find an opportunity at either the church or reception, Murphy hung around in the vicinity of the Maybelle house. With so many strangers around because of the wedding, nobody paid any attention to him. Meeting one of the wedding guests whose consumption of Pa Maybelle's Old Stump Blaster rendered talkative, Murphy pumped him for information. From the garrulous guest, he learned that the couple would spend their first night at San Antonio's best hotel and start out for their new home the following day at around noon.

In view of the way Dusty Fog's men covered the proceedings to that time, Murphy doubted if the small Texan would overlook an adequate guard over the hotel. So the killer decided against trying. While thinking that a period of inactivity on his part might lull Dusty Fog into a state of false security, Murphy learned something more.

Apparently one of Sarah Maybelle's former boyfriends was under suspicion for hiring the attempted killing of Red Blaze. The wedding guest spoke of it angrily, going into details and connecting the shooting with the arrival of the rattlesnake.

That started a fresh train of thought in Murphy's head. Until then he planned to ambush and shoot Sandy McGraw on the San Garcia trail, letting the blame fall where it would. Hearing about Finwald, Murphy changed his mind. His employer would be financially grateful for the news that the killing had been blamed on some other party. So the killer decided to make it look like the kind of amateurish job one might expect from Finwald.

After collecting his horse, Murphy rode out of San Antonio. He followed the San Garcia trail, along which the next morning

Sandy McGraw would drive with his wife. Less than a mile from town, Murphy found just what he wanted. The trail at that point had been cut into the side of a fairly steep slope. At a point where the trail made a curve stood a solitary tall tree. If the tree could be made to fall at the right moment, it ought to crash down on to the McGraws' wagon box. Even should the couple only be injured, there was a better than fair chance the panic-stricken horses would send the wagon over the lower slope.

One snag arose in the plan: timing the tree's fall. Murphy knew one way it could be arranged, although he would have to return to San Antonio and purchase the necessary equipment. While riding back to town, Murphy gave thought to another matter of vital importance: his escape after the killing. Although Anse Dale was a capable peace officer, his jurisdiction ended at San Antonio's city limits. The current sheriff of Bexar County, in which San Antonio lay, was a lethargic man who invariably took the easy course in any business. Left to himself, the sheriff would be only too pleased to accept the basic evidence: that Finwald had tried to arrange revenge himself after the failure of the previous attempts.

Unfortunately there was in San Antonio at that moment a man of driving, forceful personality, one with sufficient influential backing to force the sheriff into a thorough investigation and one capable of taking control of it himself. During the period he held a law badge in a tough Montana gold-mining town, Dusty Fog had shown considerable skill in all aspects of a peace officer's work, including the investigation of murders. The Rio Hondo gun wizard would not calmly accept the bare appearances.

If Murphy hoped to build up a big start through his false trail, he must try to make sure that Dusty Fog was not around to interfere. The obvious method, killing the small Texan, might be one answer, but Murphy did not even consider such a possibility. More than one man had tried to kill Dusty Fog and failed. The penalty for failure was death. No, Murphy had a better idea, one that was much safer yet one that he felt sure would be successful.

Returning to San Antonio, Murphy visited Finwald's store, where he purchased a hundred feet of stout Manila rope, a saw, a hammer, and a spike clamp. The latter, looking like an overgrown paper staple, was used by builders for temporarily securing two pieces of wood together. After loading his purchases onto the waiting horse, he left town once more. Eight miles from San Antonio along the San Garcia trail lay the Lone Elk stagecoach relay station. While employed by Wells Fargo, its owner augmented his salary in a number of ways that would not meet with the company's approval. For a financial consideration, the agent agreed to send a message over the telegraph wires to Dusty Fog. Maybe he even believed Murphy's story that the message was no more than a practical joke being played on the killer's wartime commanding officer. Spending the night at the relay station, Murphy reminded the agent not to send the message until noon—so that he could be in San Antonio to see the result of the joke—and rode back in that direction.

Back at the tree, the killer went to work. First he began to cut into the trunk with the saw about two feet above the ground. When the blade sank almost out of sight in the wood, Murphy took the spike clamp and drove its points into the trunk above and below the saw. Carefully he continued to cut until he saw the tree quiver and strain against the grip of the clamp. Pulling free his saw, he stood back and studied his work for a moment. Because the tree stood on a slope, it would fall downhill, so he did not need to do any branch trimming to ensure it went in the right direction. Having secured one end of the rope to the clamp, he backed off up the slope toward a large clump of mesquite some seventy-five feet from the tree. He had sufficient rope left over to lead among the bushes and fasten its other end onto his horse's saddle horn, while keeping himself and the animal hidden from the trail. All was now ready, and all Murphy had to do was wait.

Time dragged by slowly, but a man in Murphy's line of work learned the value of patience. At last he saw a two-horse wagon come into sight from the direction of San Antonio. Waiting only long enough to make sure that Sandy and Sarah McGraw rode on the wagon, Murphy went to his horse. After swinging into the saddle, he lashed the rope securely to his horn. By crouching low over the horse's neck, he could keep out of sight and turned his horse so that he was able to see the tree. While his range of vision was necessarily restricted, he saw enough to be able to judge his moves correctly.

At last the wagon approached the bend and started to turn. Murphy suddenly thrust his spurs into the horse's ribs, and the animal lunged forward. Snapping tight, the rope jerked the clamp from the tree's trunk. Freed of restraint, the tree quivered for a moment before tilting over and falling down onto the wagon. Murphy heard a startled yell from Sandy, followed by Sarah's scream and the sound of splintering timber.

Standing in the livery barn that had housed their horses during the stay in San Antonio, Betty Hardin completed saddling her mount. She looked to where her two cousins also made preparations for their departure.

"Well, Sandy and Sarah are off to their new home," she said.

"Maybe we should have gone along with them," Red remarked, drawing the double girths of his low-horned Texas saddle tight about the body of his claybank* stallion.

"Sandy didn't want it that way," Dusty pointed out, making the final adjustments to his paint's rig. "Anyways, there's been no sign of that killer around town or I'd've insisted he let us at least send Kiowa and Billy Jack along."

"Do you really think young Finwald hired him, Dusty?" Betty asked.

Before Dusty could reply, a boy entered the barn. Hero worship showed on the youngster's face, and he clearly felt that his social standing improved as a result of his delivering the buff-colored telegraph message form to the famous Dusty Fog.

"Sorry I didn't get it to you sooner, Cap'n," he stated breathlessly. "Only I took it to the hotel and they told me that you'd already left."

"Thanks, boy," Dusty answered, taking a fifteen-cent piece

* Claybank: a yellowish mixture of sorrel and dun.

from his pocket and exchanging it for the paper in the youngster's hand. "Here's a long bit for your trouble."

"Gee, thanks, Cap'n," said the boy.

Opening the form, Dusty read its message: "CAPTAIN FOG. ALAMO HOTEL. SAN ANTONIO. DUSTY. RETURN HOME IMMEDIATELY. OLE DEVIL."

"What is it, Dusty?" Betty demanded, seeing her cousin's lips tighten.

"Read it," he suggested, handing over the paper. "We're going to do some fast riding, Cousin Red."

"Grandfather never sent this!" Betty stated flatly after reading the message and passing it to Red. "He never calls you anything but Dustine, Dusty."

"I've heard him call Dusty something else." Red grinned. "Me, too."

"You both probably deserved it," Betty snorted. "Anyways, he never signs anything Ole Devil."

"It's maybe a joke," Red said in a tone that implied he did not believe the suggestion.

"The boys might play jokes, but they'd not ride out to the nearest telegraph station to send it," Dusty replied. "Where'd be the nearest place they could send a message, boy?"

"Lone Elk station out on the San Garcia trail, Cap'n," the youngster replied, his chest swelling with pride at being called upon to assist the Rio Hondo gun wizard. He could see that his information meant something to his audience.

"Let's ride, Red!" Dusty barked, taking hold of his saddle horn and vaulting astride the paint's seventeen-hands-high back.

"Look after our gear until we come back," Betty instructed the barn's owner, nodding to the loaded packhorse. "I'll come with you, Dusty."

"You go to the Bull's Head and collect Billy Jack and Kiowa," Dusty told her. "Bring them after us along the San Garcia trail."

"Yo!" answered Betty without arguing.

"Reckon that message's from the feller who tried to kill Sandy?" asked Red as he and Dusty rode from the barn.

"I'd bet on it. Who else would want us on our way home that badly?"

"Nobody I can think of offhand."

With that Red stopped speaking. Side by side the two cousins, each superbly mounted, set their horses moving at a good pace. Once clear of the town, they allowed their mounts to pick up speed. Three days resting in the livery barn, with grain feeds, made the horses eager for exercise, and they strode out fast along the San Garcia trail.

Neither Dusty nor Red wasted breath in talking until they came into sight of the wagon. Instead they concentrated on conserving their horses' energy without slackening off their pace. At last they saw Sandy's wagon ahead, approaching a corner on which grew a single tree.

"They're all ri—" Red began.

Even as he spoke, the tree quivered and began to tilt over in the direction of the passing wagon.

"What the hell—" Dusty said, for he could see no reason why the tree chose that particular moment to fall.

Then he caught sight of Murphy as the killer burst out of the bushes and galloped up the slope. Telling Red to go see to the wagon, Dusty swung his paint off the trail in the direction of the fleeing man.

While guiding his racing claybank toward the wagon, Red studied the situation. Spooked by the tree's collapse, the team horses reared and plunged, dragging the wagon toward the edge of the trail. From the trailing reins, Red concluded Sandy no longer was in any condition to control the team. So they must be halted—and fast—before they went over the edge of the slope and the wagon's weight drove them downward to destruction.

There was no time to do more than glance at the wagon's box in passing. Red saw, however, that the main weight of the tree had hit the canopy. Seeing the danger, Sandy had flung himself on top of Sarah, bearing her down and covering her with his body. They both appeared to be pinned to the seat by at least one branch, so Red could expect no help from that source.

After reining in his claybank, Red left its saddle and landed alongside the team horses. Carried forward by his impetus, he swung to face the frightened animals and lunged to their heads. Powerful hands clamped hold of each horse's reins, strong but reassuring as he fought to bring them under control. Avoiding the slashing hooves, he felt himself forced back until his heels struck the springy grass at the side of the trail.

Hooves thundered, drawing closer, and a familiar voice yelled, "Stay with it, Red!"

Up tore Betty, accompanied by Billy Jack and Kiowa. Leaving their horses at a run, the two men lit down ready to help Red halt the wagon. While Billy Jack ran forward to lend a hand with the horses, Kiowa flung himself at the wagon's brake. Riding by on her fine-looking roan, Betty gathered up the three men's horses and led them back in the direction of their owners. Once stopped, the range-bred horses could be trusted to stand without needing to be tied to anything, their trailing reins being the only inducement they needed. So Betty dropped from her saddle and ran toward the wagon.

Even with Billy Jack lending his capable assistance, Red could not have halted the horses in time had it not been for Kiowa hauling back on the brake handle. With the back wheels locked immobile, the drag of the wagon's bulk reinforced the two men's efforts and brought the team to a standstill.

"Get onto the box, you two!" Betty suggested. "I can manage them now."

"Leave 'em to me," Billy Jack answered. "They're still restless."

Realizing that Billy Jack spoke the truth, Betty did not argue. Skilled horsewoman though she undoubtedly was, the two big animals might prove too much for her should they take it into their heads to run again. So she followed Red toward the wagon box.

After applying the brake, Kiowa swung up onto the wagon box. He slid the long-bladed bowie knife from its sheath at his left side and began to hack at the branch that still held Sandy and Sarah pinned. Although the girl wriggled and struggled, Kiowa could see no sign of movement from Sandy. Cursing savagely, the lean scout increased his efforts. Only the superb quality of the knife's steel allowed it to stand up to such treatment. Wood chips flew as the shining steel bit into the branch. Then it separated from the tree, and Red helped Kiowa raise it off the newlyweds.

Almost before the branch went over the side of the wagon, Sarah wriggled out from under Sandy. Although she was frightened, her main concern was for her husband's welfare. Either when he was struck by the branch or when the spooked horses jerked the wagon, Sandy's head had struck the box hard enough to knock him unconscious. He lay limp and still, but Sarah retained sufficient control over herself not to move him.

"How is it, Sarah?" asked Red gently, standing on the box behind the girl.

"I'm all right," she replied. "See to Sandy."

"We'd best get him off the box, I reckon," Kiowa put in.

"Sure," said Red. "Reckon you can manage the team, Betty? It'll take the three of us to do it."

By that time the two horses appeared to have recovered their normal placid natures sufficiently for Betty to control them. Relieving Billy Jack, Betty kept hold of the horses' heads and remained alert for any signs of nervousness. None showed, and the removal of the unconscious Sandy went by without incident. Among them, the three men carried their still burden to a safe place and set it down. Immediately Sarah was on her knees at Sandy's side, fighting down her fears and the hysteria that threatened to make her burst into tears.

"Billy Jack, you and Kiowa get the wagon free," Betty called.

"Yo!" replied Billy Jack, and ambled over to obey.

"Let me see to Sandy, honey," Betty said to Sarah, joining the other girl. "You go and sit on the grass."

At that moment they heard the distant sound of shooting.

"Can you handle things, Cousin Betty?" Red asked, staring in the direction of the sounds.

"Well enough," she replied. "If you reckon that Dusty can't take care of himself."

"I'd say he can, most time," Red answered. "Only there're

two rifles firing up there—and Dusty doesn't have one with him."

Saying that, Red raced to his patiently waiting claybank. He went astride the horse with a bound, scooped up the reins, and started the animal moving, pointing in the direction from which the guns still roared.

7

Taking his horse up the slope at an angle that he hoped would converge with the fleeing killer's, Dusty noticed a patch of rough, uneven land dotted with prairie dog holes ahead of him. To ride a horse across such an area at speed asked for disaster. A less knowledgeable man might have gone downhill in the erroneous belief that he helped his mount. Knowing that the conformation of a horse's body lent itself better to climbing than to descending at speed, Dusty swung the horse up the slope. He passed around the danger area but in doing so lost ground on Murphy. Once clear of the prairie dog village, Dusty settled his mount into a raking, mile-devouring stride.

A hired killer often needed a good horse under him, so bought the best animal available. Murphy proved to be no exception to the rule, and his bay gelding possessed both speed and stamina. However, the bay could not start to compare to the magnificent paint stallion between Dusty's knees. Even without his weight advantage Dusty stood a better than fair chance of catching up to the killer in a long chase. Given his lighter weight and superior skill at riding, Dusty knew the chase must end successfully as long as nothing unexpected happened.

Clearly Murphy believed he had the advantage, for he turned his bay down the slope and headed for the trail. Dusty calmly held to the high ground until he could see a safe way downward. On finding what he needed, he used all his considerable skill to follow Murphy without crippling the paint or losing too much ground.

The trail wound through a wide valley, the rock-, bush-, and tree-dotted sides of which frequently hid Murphy from Dusty's sight. Not a pleasant thought when pursuing an armed and desperate man. However, Murphy never even considered turning to make a fight. As Rosa Rio claimed, Murphy was more *pistolero* than *valiente,* preferring to take as few risks as possible in his line of work. Swapping shots with the Rio Hondo gun wizard, even from ambush, did not constitute a safe and easy way of living to reach a prime old age to Murphy's way of thinking. So he concentrated on riding and making the most of his lead over the following Texan.

Despite the fact that he wore his twin Army Colts and carried a Winchester Model 1866 carbine in his saddle holster, Dusty did not start shooting. To make a hit from the back of a racing horse was possible only at close range, and in trying, one stood the chance of throwing the animal off-balance, causing it to lose speed at least or go into a dangerous stumbling fall at the worst.

Rounding a curve, the trail dipped down into a basin and rose at the other side. As he went down the slope, Murphy saw a trio of riders appear at the top of the other side. If their appearance handed Murphy a shock, his own seemed to create some consternation among them. Even as the trio reined in their horses, Murphy hauled back on the bay's mouth in an attempt to change its direction. At the same moment he recognized the center man of the trio as one of Rosa Rio's most trusted hired hands. The other two wore expensive range clothes, carried low-hanging revolvers, and sat exceptionally fine horses. On the right, tall, lean as a steer fed in the grease-wood country, a heavy mustache making a black slash across his hard face, was Starke Reynolds, rated next to the Dublin brothers at the head of the Kimble County gang. Although Murphy did not recognize the stocky youngster at Reynolds's side, he doubted if the other was a deacon traveling in disguise.

Even as Murphy identified two of the approaching trio and began to return his horse to its original route, Rosa Rio's man recognized him. Pointing down, the man yelled Murphy's name. Any thoughts the killer harbored about either enlisting the trio's aid or riding by them unhindered ended abruptly as Starke Reynolds and the youngster grabbed for and started to slide free their rifles.

Once more Murphy was forced to reconsider his position. Unless he missed his guess, Rosa had sent her man to tell of the shooting in her cantina. In that case she would have made sure that the Kimble County bunch found a target other than herself for their anger. That being so, Murphy must stand high on Starke Reynolds's list of disliked persons. Having his gang's reputation for ruthless toughness to consider, Reynolds would hardly pass up a chance to show folks what happened to those who crossed him.

Throwing back his weight in the saddle, Murphy again wrenched at the bay's reins. Confused by the conflicting orders it received, the bay fought against the bit. Instead of calming his mount, Murphy tried to drag it around, snatching brutally at its mouth. With a squeal of pain the horse reared and in doing so saved its rider's life. Up the slope, flame ripped from Reynolds's Winchester rifle. The horse reared straight into the bullet meant for Murphy, gave a single scream, crumpled, and fell. Feeling it going down, Murphy threw a leg across his saddle and hurled himself clear. He missed death for a second time as the youngster cut loose with his .50-caliber Sharp's carbine, its bullet passing through the space occupied an instant before by Murphy's leaping body. Two strides carried Murphy off the trail, and the Winchester crashed again, missing him as he dived behind the nearest rock large enough to offer adequate protection against his assailants.

While hidden from the Kimble County men, Murphy knew himself to be far from out of danger. In fact, his position rapidly went from bad to worse. Behind him, the clatter of fast-moving hooves heralded the arrival of yet another enemy. Twisting his head around without exposing himself to Starke Reynolds's party, Murphy saw Dusty Fog race into view on the trail to his rear.

Any pleasure that Dusty might have felt at seeing the killer pinned down and left afoot died abruptly. Possibly Starke Reynolds would have drawn the correct conclusion from Dusty's hurried arrival, remembering that Murphy had been in full flight when first seen, but his young companion never gave the matter a thought. Slipping another bullet into the Sharp's carbine's chamber, Mack Potter aimed and fired at the small cowhand, the bullet sending Dusty's Stetson spinning from his head. Instantly Dusty left his horse, landing on the edge of the trail and allowing his impetus to carry him into cover. Wise in such matters, the big paint swerved off the trail as it felt its master's weight removed from the saddle. Going off to one side, it slowed down and stopped outside the danger area.

Landing on the ground behind the trunk of a tree, Dusty already held a Colt in his right hand. However, he knew himself to be at a considerable disadvantage in the matter. He did not know who Murphy's attackers might be but guessed that they were unlikely to regard his own presence favorably. In the matter of raising objections, the men across the basin held a considerable edge. At a range of maybe two hundred yards, a rifle licked even the long-barreled Army Colt in the matter of the accurate placing of its bullets.

Regretfully Dusty glanced toward his paint as it stood patiently some distance from the trail and almost level with Murphy's hiding place. The brown butt of his Winchester Model 1866 carbine showed from the saddle holster but might just as well have been left at the OD Connected for all the good it did him so far away.

In addition to practicing a fast draw and close-range accuracy with his matched Colts, Dusty had spent time learning how to shoot over distances more suited to either a carbine or rifle. By resting his elbows on the ground, shooting from the prone position, and supporting his right hand with the left, Dusty could hope to aim and eventually hit one of his assailants. However, doing so meant remaining in the same position and exposed to the return fire of his target and the second man on the rim. As soon as the trio saw Murphy take cover, Rosa Rio's employee took all the horses back over the rim and remained with them. So Dusty would have only two attackers to consider, unless he counted Murphy, but they were one too many to allow careful shooting over such a range.

Another point Dusty had to consider was the standing of the two men who halted Murphy. It could be that they were honest travelers who saw the chase and stopped a man they believed to be a criminal. Even the shot fired at Dusty proved nothing as it could have been sent off by a youngster wild with excitement and unthinking as a result of it.

Any further thoughts Dusty might have had on the subject ended as Murphy saw a possible way out of a real tight spot.

"Hey, Fog! Dusty Fog!" the killer called. "Them two up there're the Kimble County boys and're planning a robbery. If you want to know who hired me to kill McGraw, you'll have to get them off my trail."

The words not only reached Dusty but carried to the ears of Reynolds and his companion. A cold, quick grin of bitter appreciation crossed Dusty's lips. All too well he understood the reason for the shouted speech. Caught between two enemies, Murphy hoped to set them against each other. If they did not wipe each other out, he might escape while they fought. Murphy knew that Dusty wanted the name of his employer badly enough to face the Kimble County men to obtain it. Even if the small Texan did not, Reynolds would not wish to have him alive and in possession of the knowledge, especially when his gang planned a robbery of such magnitude that they had to obtain aid from the Hole-in-the-Wall bunch.

So Starke Reynolds would try to kill Dusty, that was for sure. Equally certain was that the only way the small cowhand could reach Murphy was by taking chances. Dusty intended that they be calculated risks.

Suddenly Dusty flung himself out of cover, bounding in a swerving dash for a large rock some feet closer to Murphy's position. His movement took both men by surprise. Although both Winchester and Sharp's cracked, their bullets missed Dusty's racing body, and before the men could reload, he landed behind the rock. In cover once more, he looked around and selected his next move. To the right stood a large and substantial rock, within easy distance for an unexpected rush, except that the two outlaws would figure on his making for it. On his left, the nearest cover was a small clump of bushes, not the kind of place one would choose under more favorable conditions.

Having decided which way the men expected him to go, Dusty went the other. Darting to the left, he reached the cover of the bushes before either Reynolds or Potter managed to correct his aim. Near the bushes a shallow depression offered better protection, and Dusty rolled into it. He found that by keeping down, he could move in the required direction. Up the slope, Reynolds and Potter exchanged curses as they scoured the ground ahead of them and failed to locate Dusty's position.

Cautiously the small Texan eased himself up the side of the depression, picking a point between two smallish rocks that offered a clear view of the two outlaws. When no bullet came, Dusty guessed they had not seen him. Then he looked to where Murphy crouched, not ten yards away.

"Throw your gun out here, Murphy!" Dusty called, just loud enough for the killer to hear him. "Make a move to show them where I am and I'll blow your head off."

A shocked thrill ran through Murphy at the sound of Dusty's voice. While the Kimble County boys could not see the hired killer, he must be in plain view of Dusty Fog and within what to the Rio Hondo gun wizard was easy revolver shot. Then another thought hit Murphy with shocking impact. It seemed that Rosa Rio sold him out on all sides, for the small Texan had used his name. Not that it would matter if Murphy's escape plan worked—or failed.

To make the plan work, Murphy must lure Dusty Fog up close, and that meant complying with the order to throw away his revolver. After slipping the Allen & Wheelock from its holster, he threw it well clear of his position. While doing so, his eyes flickered to the patiently waiting paint stallion. With that fast, powerful animal between his knees, Murphy knew he could outrun the two owlhoots. He felt certain enough of it to gamble on reaching the horse, although that meant running the gauntlet of Reynolds's and Potter's weapons. Only to reach the horse, Dusty Fog had to be dead.

Clearly Dusty did not intend to rush blindly forward. With his Colt gripped in both hands, he sighted carefully up the slope. Neither of the outlaws appeared to be taking any great precautions, having seen that Dusty did not hold a rifle when he quit the paint's saddle. Although lying down, they left themselves exposed in a casual manner. Using all his skill and knowledge, Dusty lined his Colt. At that moment as on other, less dangerous, occasions, he wished that Colonel Sam had fitted the Army Colt with a better rear sight than the notch cut into its hammer's lip. Taken with the low blade foresight, the V-shaped nick did not make for an accurate sight picture.

When sure that his aim could not be improved, Dusty squeezed the trigger. He felt the Colt buck in his hands, and powder smoke blotted his vision. The bullet's arrival came as a complete surprise to both Kimble County owlhoots, especially to Reynolds. Suddenly lead struck the rock behind which he lay partially hidden and flung chips of it into his face.

Dropping his rifle, spluttering curses and grabbing at his face, Reynolds still retained sufficient control of himself to think and give orders.

"Watch him, Mack! He aims to make another move!"

"Who'd you want, Fog or Murphy?" Potter asked.

"Eith—"

Before Reynolds could finish his words, Dusty left the depression and hurled himself toward where Murphy crouched. Potter cursed as he suddenly became conscious of his carbine's inadequacy. With only one shot available, he did not want to shoot unless sure of making a hit.

A low hiss of triumph broke from Murphy as he saw Dusty dashing toward him. Dropping his right hand, the killer slid the thin-bladed Arkansas toothpick from its booth sheath. Then he waited, tense and ready, watching Dusty come closer.

It took even a good rifle shot around four seconds to make an aimed discharge at a running target. Bearing that in mind, Dusty counted the seconds as he ran. Then he remembered the knife Murphy carried and realized the danger it put him in. There would be no time to change direction or find fresh cover. So Dusty did not try. Instead he made a jumping slide, going rump down along the ground like a baseball player trying to slide home and beat the ball. Up rose Murphy's arm, the knife held Indian-fashion for a downward stab. Only before he could send the knife on its way, he saw Dusty's body twist. Driving up his right leg, Dusty smashed the bottom of his foot into Murphy's face. Even from such an awkward position, the kick packed enough force to slam Murphy backward. Before the man could stop himself, he reeled from behind the rock. Up the slope Potter changed his aim and fired at Murphy as the killer crashed to the ground. Caught in the body by a .50-caliber Sharp's bullet, Murphy slammed over, screamed, and lay kicking in agony.

"Get one of them?" demanded Reynolds, rubbing his eyes clear of tears.

"Murphy," Potter replied. "He rolled like a gut-shot rabbit."

"Where's Fog?"

"Behind the rock Murphy was using."

Joining his companion, Reynolds studied the situation and assessed it. Usually where Dusty Fog was, there could be found Mark Counter and the Ysabel Kid. If that pair of handy jaspers should be anywhere within hearing range, they would be headed to their amigo's aid. That meant that time did not exist for an extended shoot-out.

"I'll keep him there," Reynolds said. "You move off along the slope until you can get a clear shot at him."

"Sure, Starke," Potter replied eagerly.

"And don't take fool chances," Reynolds warned. "You're not safe from that damned Colt even this far off."

A point Potter did not need reminding about. Not a prudent young man, he still possessed sufficient caution to avoid stupid chances when dealing with somebody like Dusty Fog. Yet as he moved along under the cover of the rim, Potter felt sure that his presence was unsuspected by the intended victim.

In that Potter made a mistake and underestimated Dusty's ability to follow an enemy's line of thought. Knowing how most people expected his two companions to be around wherever he might be, Dusty figured that the outlaws ought to make some move before Mark and the Kid came onto the scene. With that decided, one did not need great military genius to guess at the next move in the game. Knowing what the outlaws planned, Dusty sought a means of countering them.

Once again he glanced with regret at the butt of his carbine. If he could only lay hands on the little saddle gun, the affair would take on a different complexion. Unfortunately the paint stood too far away for him to reach it in a single dash, and he did not wish to endanger it by drawing attention to the carbine. Even if his attackers decided he offered too chancy a target, they might shoot the paint and hope it fell onto the saddle holster, so preventing him from obtaining a means to counter their superior-ranged weapons.

Then Dusty brought back his eyes to Murphy's dead horse. It lay on its right flank and not far from his position. In common with most western men, the killer carried his rifle booted on the left side and favored the system of pointing it in a rearward direction. So there, exposed to Dusty's gaze, lay the means to equal his enemies' armament—if he could only reach it.

Glancing up the slope, Dusty noticed that only Reynolds remained in the original position. That meant that the other owlhoot sought a place offering an unrestricted line of fire onto the small Texan. At any moment a bullet might come crashing into Dusty from the Sharp's carbine. A further state of urgency came as Murphy stirred and moaned.

"A—a doctor, for Gawd's sake!" the killer gasped.

The movement drew Reynolds's attention to Murphy, and Dusty saw the Kimble County man's rifle alter its aim. Instantly the small Texan hurled himself from behind the rock and toward the dead horse. Taken by surprise, Reynolds jerked his Winchester back in an attempt to take sight on Dusty. Already set to shoot at Murphy, his finger squeezed the trigger, and the bullet flew harmlessly down to kick dirt up on the trail. Before Reynolds could lever home another bullet, Dusty leaped over the horse's body. In passing he gripped the butt of the rifle and slid it from the saddle holster. Having landed beyond the animal, Dusty twisted around and behind its body. He threw forward the rifle's lever and fed a round into the chamber—or hoped he did, for he had no way of knowing if the magazine was loaded. Few men, especially those following Murphy's trade, carried an empty rifle, so Dusty felt he could safely assume the one in his hands held at least some bullets. Carefully Dusty began to move himself up behind the horse, easing the borrowed Winchester ahead of him.

Having reached a place from which he could cover the previously hidden side of the rock, Potter saw Dusty vacate it and started to raise his carbine.

"Drop it!" shouted a voice.

Swinging in the direction of the speaker, Potter saw a tall redheaded cowhand wearing an eye-catching red and white vest standing not thirty yards away. With a snarl of rage, the outlaw turned his carbine in the direction of the newcomer, sighted fast, and fired.

Although eager to reach Dusty, Red Blaze knew better than to charge headlong down the trail. Instead he left his horse standing out of sight and advanced on foot. Nor did he intend to rely upon his Colts, but held a Spencer carbine at the ready. Searching the ground ahead of him, Red saw the threat to his cousin's life and yelled a challenge.

Whipping up his Spencer, undeterred by the sound of Potter's bullet hissing by his face, Red snapped off a shot and also missed. Immediately they both started to reload. Each gun worked on the same basic principle. Lowering the lever which served as a trigger guard opened the breech and ejected the empty cartridge case. At that point the Spencer's action differed from that of the single-shot Sharp's. The spring feed of the magazine thrust the next .52-caliber bullet into the chamber instead of its user's needing to drop it home by hand. Returning the lever to perform its secondary function of trigger guard left only the need to thumb-cock the hammer before making all ready to fire again. (One of the reasons the otherwise excellent Spencer repeaters failed was that their inventor designed them with the breech and lock mechanisms operating separately.)

The need for thumb cocking prevented the Spencer from being appreciably faster than a well-served Sharp's carbine, but the slight edge in speed proved to be sufficient. As Potter started to draw back his Sharp's hammer, Red aimed and squeezed the Spencer's trigger. Under the circumstances Red shot the only way he dared, to kill. Give a hardened young outlaw like the one before him half a chance, and there would be no hesitation in the way he acted. So Red drove a bullet between Potter's eyes and tumbled him over the edge of the rim to roll down the slope.

When he heard the fresh burst of shots and saw his companion's downward roll, Starke Reynolds decided the time had come to yell calf rope and quit. From the rag-doll, limp manner in which Potter moved, Reynolds knew he was dead or so close to it as made no difference. That would be all to the good, for dead men gave no information. Swiftly Reynolds backed from the rim and, when sure Dusty could not see him, rose to make good his escape. He ran to where Rosa Rio's man waited with the horses and snatched his mount's reins from the other's hand.

"Where's the young one?" the man asked.

"Cashed in!" Reynolds replied. "Tell Rosa the job's off. It's been a damned sight too unlucky so far for it to go right."

With that Starke Reynolds mounted his horse and galloped off in the direction from which he had come. Dusty Fog would never learn the objective of the big robbery that called for the services of two powerful gangs, for it never happened.

8

A groan from Murphy, mingled with the sound of departing hooves beyond the rim, brought Dusty to his feet. Tense and watchful, the small Texan stood for a moment looking around. Then he heard Red's voice.

"How many of 'em, Cousin Dusty?"

"I've only seen two."

"The other one just lit out then," Red commented.

"Sounds that way," Dusty said, listening to two distinct sets of hooves fading away.

After shoving the rifle back into the saddle holster Dusty went to Murphy's side and bent down. The Sharp's bullet had caught the killer in the back, just missing the spine. Being made of solid lead, it ranged through the man's chest cavity with a terrible mushrooming effect. Although Murphy still lived, it would be only a matter of time before death claimed him. Nothing could save the man with such a wound, so Dusty decided to learn as much as he could about the attempts on Sandy McGraw's life.

"Murphy," he said quietly, "who hired you?"

Slowly the killer turned his face and looked through pain-creased eyes at Dusty. "A—a priest. I . . . want . . . a . . . priest."

"And I'll see you get to one," Dusty assured him. "Who paid you to kill Sandy McGraw?"

"I—I . . . only want a priest," Murphy mumbled.

Having made sure that nothing could be done for the man he shot, Red joined his cousin in time to hear the last answer. Both of them had seen enough of the Catholic border dwellers to know the futility of asking further questions.

"He'll tell us nothing, Cousin Dusty," Red stated.

"That's for sure," Dusty replied.

"Shall I take out after that jasper who got away?"

"Let him go, Red. He's got too good a start on you and won't be back."

At that moment they heard hooves drumming on the trail and turned to see Billy Jack galloping up. After bringing his horse to a halt, the lean cowhand dropped out of the saddle. An expression of relief flickered across his doleful face at finding Dusty safe and unharmed. Then he looked down at the groaning killer.

"So this's him, Cap'n Dusty."

"This's him," Dusty answered. "Are Sarah and Sandy hurt?"

"Gal's a mite shook up but not hurt," Billy Jack replied. "Sandy shoved her down and laid over her so that the tree hit him. Got a couple of bust ribs, and his shoulder's cracked. The boss lady said I should come and see if you pair needed any help."

"We need some," Dusty stated. "Is the wagon damaged?"

"Just the canopy."

"Go bring it here. We're toting him in with us."

"Yo!" Billy Jack answered, needing no more detailed instructions or any explanations. After collecting his waiting horse, he mounted and rode off to carry out Dusty's orders.

"You'd better get afork that off-yellow crowbait and burn grass to San Antonio, Cousin Red," Dusty went on. "Have the sheriff send out for that yahoo's body. But before you do it, send word to the mission and ask for one of the fathers to meet the wagon when it comes in."

"I'll see to it," Red promised. "Reckon you'll be all right here?"

"Sure. That jasper who lit out won't stop running until he hits Kimble County again. Besides, Murphy may say something."

For all his easy assurance, Dusty took the precaution of bringing his paint to the edge of the trail and slipping his Winchester carbine from its saddle holster. If he should need a weapon, he preferred one he knew rather than a borrowed gun of uncertain performance. Resting the carbine against the dead horse's rump, he did what little he could to make Murphy comfortable.

While waiting for the wagon's arrival, Dusty listened to Murphy's pain-induced mutterings. He hoped to learn who hired Murphy to kill Sandy McGraw but did not. Instead the killer talked incoherently of Rosa Rio's treachery, some girl he knew below the border, and, to Dusty's surprise, the legend of Jim Bowie's lost mine.

Deciding that pain caused Murphy's mind to wander, Dusty ignored what he heard. The girl meant nothing to him, and he had witnessed part of Rosa Rio's betrayal, so he did not doubt she also passed word to the Kimble County gang. As for the old legend, Dusty knew it all too well.

According to the story, Jim Bowie discovered a fabulous silver mine while hunting wild horses in the days before Texas broke away from Mexico. War came before the great knife fighter could exploit his find, and he took the secret of the mine's location with him when he died at the Alamo. Since all his companions from the wild-horse hunt also perished in the fighting that cost Mexico a province and eventually gave the United States the state, nobody knew where the mine might be.

Of course, people searched for it, as they always will for the pot of gold at the end of the rainbow and with no more success.

In fact, selling "genuine" maps showing the mine's location exceeded the disposal of "real" gold bricks as the top stock-in-trade of Texas confidence tricksters.

Murphy did not strike Dusty as being the kind of man to fall for such a hoary trick, although some surprising people had been taken in by it. Possibly the killer had made money from it on occasion and wished the fact to be taken into consideration at confession along with his other sins.

Before Dusty could form any conclusions, the wagon arrived. After turning it to point in the direction of San Antonio, Kiowa jumped down to help load Murphy into the rear. On first hearing what Dusty required, Sarah had objected to letting the killer ride with his victim. However, Betty had persuaded the other girl that Dusty acted for the best, stating that Murphy alone could tell them who hired him. So Sarah raised no opposition as the men placed the wounded Murphy in the wagon.

Once more Kiowa drove the team, while Betty went inside to help Sarah and also to listen should Murphy make any statement regarding his attempts to kill the young couple. Already Murphy was sinking fast, and the girl wondered if he would live to see the priest Red had raced to collect and would have waiting in town.

"Did he say anything, Cap'n Dusty?" Billy Jack asked as they rode ahead of the wagon.

"Nope," Dusty answered.

"You reckon it was that Finwald *hombre* hired him?"

"It could have been," Dusty admitted. "But I'm beginning to doubt it."

"Any good reason for you doing that?" Billy Jack wanted to know.

"Nothing more than a hunch."

"I for sure hope we learn one way or the other," the lean cowhand said miserably. "Some of the boys are plenty riled up about that snake and the shooting. When they hear about this game, they'll likely start reaching for a rope."

"Then you tell them I said for them to put it down again," Dusty growled.

"Aw, shucks, Cap'n Dusty, he's only a Republican."

"There's a law against hanging folks informal like," Dusty reminded his former sergeant major. *"Even* Republicans."

"Damned if I can see why, there's too many of 'em about anyways." Billy Jack sniffed. Then his voice took on a more serious note. "Like I said, Cap'n Dusty, feelings're running plenty high in town. Sandy's real well liked, and young Finwald ain't."

"Only having Finwald as guest of honor at a cottonwood hoedown isn't going to settle anything," Dusty pointed out.

"It'd settle him," Billy Jack replied.

"And won't help any," Dusty insisted. "Especially if it comes out later that he's innocent."

Dusty believed that he could hold the men in check, even though most of them did not work for the OD Connected. Yet things might go wrong. He had to return to his home in the near future, and after his departure a wrong word when the whiskey flowed could bring the whole business to a boil again. So Dusty wanted the affair straightened out before he left San Antonio. Everything depended on the man dying in the back of the wagon. He alone could clear, or incriminate, Finwald if he wished.

On approaching the outskirts of the town, Dusty saw that Red had acted with customary efficiency. A doctor and a priest stood with the redhead, looking toward the wagon. Riding up to the waiting men, Dusty told them quickly what had happened and why he sent to them. Without wasting time, the doctor and the gray-haired priest entered the wagon. Kiowa started the team moving once more, driving the horses at a fast walk through the town in the direction of Sarah's house. As they passed the Bull's Head Saloon, one of Sandy's friends looked out. He spoke over his shoulder, shoved open the batwing doors, and stepped through. Accompanied by a growing crowd, the cowhand followed the wagon.

Betty jumped from the rear of the wagon as it halted and went to where her cousins dismounted by the picket fence.

"Murphy's going fast," she said. "The doctor claims there's no chance of him leaving the wagon alive."

Track Down And Capture Exciting Western Adventure!
WANTED!
LOUIS L'AMOUR COLLECTION!
REWARD OFFERED
Mail your "WANTED" poster today. (see inside)
Make your "wanted" claim and receive your rightful reward!
• A free authentic Louis L'Amour calendar!
• A free preview of the bestselling SACKETT
And much more...

THE LOUIS L'AMOUR COLLECTION

It's a Louis L'Amour Free Offer!

This exciting, no-risk offer lets you sample from one of America's most gifted storytellers — without obligation!

HERE'S WHAT YOU GET:

1. **FREE!** We'll send you the latest Louis L'Amour wall calendar *free*. With 13 full-page, four-color paintings from the covers of 13 Louis L'Amour works. This is a *free gift* to cherish, throughout the year and beyond. And remember it's yours to keep, *without obligation*.

2. **FREE PREVIEW!** Louis L'Amour has almost 200 million books in print. He's had 30 of his stories made into movies or television shows. Now *without obligation*, you can sample SACKETT, one of the most popular novels from "Our professor emeritus of how the west was won" (Morley Safer on "60 Minutes"). Keep SACKETT for 15 days — read and enjoy it. If after 15 days you decide Louis L'Amour is not for you — simply return SACKETT and owe nothing.

3. **EXCLUSIVE VALUE!** If Louis L'Amour is for you, *The Louis L'Amour Collection* offers you exclusive value that can't be matched. This special collector's edition:

- is not available in bookstores anywhere
- each 6¼" x 9¼" volume is handsomely bound in rich, rugged sierra-brown simulated leather.
- the title and L'Amour signature are embossed in gold on the spine and cover.

And best of all you pay only $10.95 (plus shipping and handling) for each luxurious volume.

4. **NO OBLIGATION!** But remember there is no obligation. Sample SACKETT free for 15 days — return it and owe nothing. The magnificent wall calendar is yours to keep — regardless. If you keep SACKETT pay just $10.95 and start your *Louis L'Amour Collection*. Sample a different Louis L'Amour once a month — always with 15 days to preview — always with the right to cancel anytime.

Enter the world of Louis L'Amour adventure today — mail your "WANTED" sticker and free offer card today.

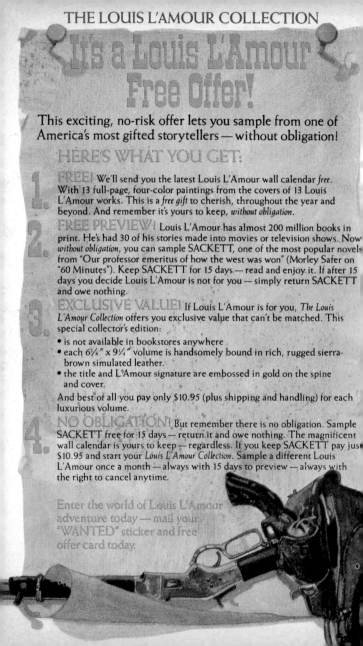

FREE — MAGNIFICENT WALL CALENDAR!
FREE — PREVIEW OF SACKETT
- No Obligation! • No Purchase Necessary!

Yes! I'm claiming my reward!

Send SACKETT for 15 days free! If I keep this volume, I will pay just $10.95 plus shipping and handling. Future Louis L'Amour Westerns will be sent to me about once a month, on a 15-day, Free-Examination basis. I understand that there is no minimum number of books to buy and I may cancel my subscription at any time. The Free Louis L'Amour wall calendar is mine to keep even if I decide to return SACKETT.

"WANTED!"
STICKER
GOES HERE

NAME _____

ADDRESS _____

CITY _____

STATE _____ ZIP _____

MY NO RISK GUARANTEE:

There's no obligation to buy. The free calendar is mine to keep. I may preview SACKETT and any other Louis L'Amour book for 15 days. If I don't want it, I simply return the book and owe nothing. If I keep it, I pay only $10.95 (plus postage and handling).

IL2

70136

Track down and capture exciting western adventure from one of America's foremost novelists!

• It's free! • No obligation! • Exclusive value!

"We'd best get Sandy and Sarah out of it then," Dusty stated. "Let's go, Red, Billy Jack."

"Sure," Red answered. "Has he said anything, Betty?"

"Nothing that makes sense," the girl admitted, watching Billy Jack fasten her horse alongside Dusty's paint after leading it in for her. "He's going fast, and there's not much time."

Working swiftly under the doctor's guidance, Red, Billy Jack, Kiowa, and Sarah's father—the latter having come from the house on seeing the wagon's unexpected return—carried Sandy to a place where his injuries could receive more adequate treatment. Sarah allowed Dusty to help her down and ran after her husband. Then Dusty looked into the rear of the wagon where the priest started to kneel at the dying man's side. Meeting Dusty's inquiring gaze, the priest shook his head and turned his attention once more to Murphy.

"It won't be long now," Dusty told Betty.

"No," she replied. "We've got company, Cousin Dusty."

Much as Dusty wanted to learn the identity of Murphy's employer, the thought that he might do so by eavesdropping on the killer's dying confession never entered his head. He was already prepared to withdraw out of hearing distance, and the arrival of Sandy's friends gave him a greater reason for doing so.

"Who done it, Cap'n?" demanded a brawny young cowhand in the lead of the party.

"The same feller who tried before," Dusty replied. "A hired gun called Murphy."

"He around?"

"In the wagon—and stopping there."

The crowd's advance came to a halt. Practically every man in it had served under Dusty's command during the war and knew that when his voice took on that clipped, incisive note, it was time to sit back and listen with both ears. Although a number of hostile glances flashed in the direction of the wagon, none of the men made any attempt to approach it.

"Thing now being who hired this Murphy *hombre*," remarked a second man. "His sort's not pulling those kind of games for fun."

"You know who hired him, Cap'n?" growled the first speaker.

"Not yet," Dusty admitted.

"Maybe you ain't asked him right," said the brawny cowhand.

"Could be, Tule," Dusty said quietly.

"We could ask," Tule went on.

"But *we* won't!" Dusty stated flatly, recalling other occasions during the war when he had needed to take a firm line to control the brawny cowhand.

"He tried to kill Sandy," Tule pointed out.

"I know that," Dusty replied. "And I know he's dying in there. A priest's with him, and *nobody's* going to interfere."

Silence, broken only by an occasional low mutter, fell over the crowd. They stood studying the wagon, but none offered to move beyond the small man who was between it and them. At last the priest dropped to the ground and looked in Dusty's direction.

"It's over, Dusty," Betty said, for her cousin's attention remained on the crowd before him.

"I'll see what the priest has to say," Dusty replied. "You boys just stay put for a whiles longer."

"The war's long over," Tule muttered as Dusty turned away. "We don't have to take his orders no more."

"You fixing on telling *him* so?" asked a leathery old-timer dryly.

On giving the matter some rapid thought, Tule decided not to comment on it. Maybe Captain Fog no longer had the backing of the Confederate States Army's disciplinary machinery, but he had rarely relied upon it even when having it available. Nor did anything in his record since the war lead Tule to believe Dusty would no longer employ the very effective methods by which he had dealt with disobedient or unruly soldiers.

"I just figured we ought to do something about Sandy," Tule finally claimed.

"So do we," drawled the old-timer. "And happen Cap'n Dusty'll tell us what and when we do it."

"Can I speak to you, Father?" Dusty asked, joining Betty and walking up to the priest.

"Of course."

"The man in the wagon tried to kill Sandy and Sarah McGraw."

"So your young friend told the doctor while we waited for you to arrive," the priest said, speaking excellent English despite his Mexican birth.

"I want to learn why and who hired him to do it," Dusty went on.

"I'm sorry, Captain Fog," the priest said. "But I can't tell you that."

"This's *real* important, Father," Dusty said. "You see those men there? Every one of them is Sandy's friend. They reckon they know who hired Murphy and aim to get even for Sandy. I'd hate like he—I'd sure hate to see an innocent man suffer."

"And if the one they suspect is guilty?"

"You can rely on Dusty to see that *legal* justice takes its course, Father," Betty put in. "I realize that you cannot violate the sacred rite of confession, but we must know if Chester Finwald did hire that man."

"He did not," stated the priest.

"Murphy told you that?" the girl asked.

"He told me. You see, I've heard about this business and made a point of learning what it was about. While young Finwald is not of our people, I felt I should try to learn the truth."

"Would Murphy tell you the truth, Father?" Red asked, having rejoined his cousins when he saw the crowd arrive and stood in the background ready to back up Dusty's play if needed.

"A dying man doesn't lie, my son," the priest assured him. "Especially one with many sins on his conscience."

"If it wasn't Finwald, who did hire him?" Red asked.

"I can't tell you that," the priest answered.

"Murphy didn't tell you?" Red demanded.

"No. He said only that Finwald was not the one."

"Thanks for your help, Father," Dusty said.

"I wish I could do more," the priest replied. "Now I will make arrangements for his burial."

"Sure, Father," Dusty said. "I'd admire to search his property if I can."

"That will be a matter between yourself and the marshal," the priest said.

"If Murphy hasn't enough money for the burial—" Betty began.

"I understand," the priest told her.

While the conversation had been taking place, the crowd drew slowly closer. Turning toward them, Dusty said, "Finwald's not the one, boys. You may as well go back to whatever you were doing."

"How'd you know for sure it wasn't him?" demanded Tule.

After stepping by Dusty, Red thrust his face close to the brawny cowhand. "Tule, you never had one lick of good sense, but try to get some and *pronto*. You've pushed Cousin Dusty just about as far as any one man can without wishing he hadn't *real* rapid. Now my advice to you'd be go back, drink your drink, have your fun, but leave thinking to them with something in their heads to do it."

Having learned the hard way that Red fought only slightly less effectively than his cousin, Tule swallowed any objections he felt at the words. A glance around showed him that the remainder of the crowd accepted Dusty's advice and that they were starting to drift away. Then the old-timer stepped forward.

"Asking your pardon, and not doubting you any, Cap'n Dusty," he said, "but you wouldn't know who *did* hire that jasper?"

"Nope," Dusty admitted. "But I aim to find out."

The statement appeared to satisfy the majority of the crowd. Even Tule raised no more dissent but turned and walked away with the rest. Having listened to her cousin and watched his handling of what might easily have been a tricky situation, Betty let the men go before raising a point that puzzled her.

"Just how do you aim to find out, cousin, dear?"

"Trust a woman to ask fool questions," Red put in. "How are you fixing to do it, Dusty?"

"Way I see is this," Dusty answered. "First off there's only one man around here with reason to want Sandy dead, and he didn't hire Murphy—"

"Unless Murphy lied," Red drawled, "which I don't think he did either."

"So you think maybe it's somebody up San Garcia way behind Murphy?" Betty asked, acting as if Red did not exist.

"Like somebody said," Dusty replied. "Sandy never owned a ranch before. Or will, if he pays off the back taxes on it by noon of the tenth."

"Somebody would want the ranch pretty bad to hire a killer to stop Sandy claiming it," Betty commented. "And why would he want Sarah dead?"

"Sandy wouldn't go up there so soon if she had been," Dusty replied. "Or maybe Murphy heard about Finwald and thought up a good way to throw the blame away from his boss."

"What're we going to do about it, Dusty?" Red asked.

Before Dusty could reply, the house door flew open and Sarah came out. Running along the path, she halted in front of the cousins. Her face was a mixture of relief and concern.

"Cap'n Dusty," she gasped, "Sandy's recovered—"

"*Bueno*—" Dusty began.

"It's not good!" Sarah replied, almost in tears. "The doctor says he mustn't travel for at least a week. So we won't be able to reach San Garcia in time to pay the back taxes. We'll lose the ranch if Sandy isn't there."

"Don't you worry none on that score," Dusty told her, darting a glance at Red. "Sandy's going to be there."

Guessing what Dusty planned to do, Betty smiled and laid a hand on Sarah's arm. "And so are you, honey."

"I won't leave Sandy!" Sarah stated.

"You'll be in San Garcia just the same," Betty said.

Part Two
The Man Behind the Hired Gun

9

Never had the town of San Garcia seethed with such suppressed excitement, not even when one of the local spreads returned from a trail drive to the Kansas railhead market. Normally a sleepy collection of wood or adobe houses and business premises scattered haphazardly close to the Rio Moreno, it showed a bubbling eagerness that hinted at big doings in the near future. Many of its citizens had already gathered in the central plaza and were waiting for what ought to be a time to be remembered. Fastened in prominent positions around town and scattered widely across the surrounding countryside, notices announced the sale of the McGraw ranch to offset lapsed taxes.

Everybody in town knew full well that Cal Mobstell of the Rocking Rafter outfit wanted to add the McGraw place to his not inconsiderable holdings. Nor was it any great secret that Francisco Cordova hoped that day to increase the size of his already large Whangdoodle ranch and augment its resources

with Seth McGraw's water. Since each rancher possessed sufficient wealth, and the backing of loyal, hardy men, to gain his
way in most matters, the auction ought to prove interesting, to
say the least.

Already Cordova's Mexican crew had gathered in the
Paraiso cantina; but the band did not play, and the flashing-
eyed senoritas of easy virtue remained in their rooms. Down at
the other end of the plaza, in the Golden Goose saloon, Mobstell and four of his cowhands sat sipping beer in a silence,
made the more menacing when compared to their usual rowdy
behavior in town. Every ingredient was on hand for a hell of a
ruckus, the only requirement being somebody to start stirring
up the pot.

Feeling like a cook preparing a stew of gunpowder and dyna-
mite, Herbert Corlin, the county land agent, came down from
his room on the saloon's first floor. Small, thin, wearing an
expensive town suit, Corlin gave the impression of being a cow-
ardly weasel. He jumped nervously as he saw Mobstell rise and
walk toward him, yet the bulky rancher's broad face bore a
friendly grin.

"How's about starting that sale, Herb?" asked the rancher.

"It's not a quarter to twelve yet," Corlin answered.

"So what difference's fifteen minutes or so going to make?"
snorted Mobstell. "Let's get her started and done with."

"I've no legal right to sell until noon," Corlin protested. "Up
until that time Seth McGraw's heir's got the right to come in,
pay off the back taxes, and take possession."

"There's been no sight nor sound of him yet," Mobstell answered. "He's not likely to be coming now."

"You seem to be in one big hurry to get the sale started," said
a voice from the main batwing doors of the saloon.

Slowly Mobstell turned to look at the newcomer. The
rancher was a big man, heavily built, powerful, dressed in
much the same style and quality clothing as his hired hands.
Around his waist hung a gun belt with an Army Colt in its
holster. He looked like just the kind of man he was. Tough,
capable, he had come to Texas in the early days with little or
nothing. Hard work, guts, and willingness to accept the respon-

sibilities of ownership had lifted him over those content to remain as employees. Such a man did not lightly turn aside once he had made up his mind on a course of action.

Compared to Mobstell, the newcomer appeared almost effeminately groomed. A costly white sombrero sat on his head. Unlike Mobstell's bristle-covered features, his handsome face was smoothly shaved. His charro outfit of soft brown leather, with a decorative filigree of silver, and white shirt showed no signs of wear, while the gun belt and boots bore a polish almost good enough to reflect the scenery. Francisco Cordova was tall and slim and moved with a bullfighter's grace. However, he did not rely on a matador's weapons. In the contoured holster of his gun belt, just right for a fast draw, rode a magnificent Colt 1861 Navy revolver with a fancy solid silver Tiffany butt of the kind popular among Mexican dandies. Elegant dresser Cordova might be, but he had built his ranch in the same way as Mobstell, by hard work, cold courage, and being ready, willing, and able to fight for his rights.

"There's some of us work our spreads instead of hiring the sweating done," Mobstell replied. "So we can't spend too much time in town."

At their table Mobstell's companions stirred in their seats. Bob Lynn, six feet of whang leather toughness; Shanty, middle-sized yet strong; Avon, black-bearded and big; Luke Clayd, tall, young, and capable: a quartet ready to fight at the drop of a hat and knock it down themselves. Although none of them moved, they watched their boss, ready to back any play he made.

Tension crackled in the air. Behind Cordova, outside the batwing doors, stood four Mexican vaqueros. No less tough or willing than the Rocking Rafter men, they needed only their patron's order to set them going. One wrong word, a single hasty action, and the town would see its excitement even before the sale started.

Standing at the long mahogany bar, Tony Towcester watched the scene. As owner of the saloon he had more than a casual interest in what developed. His property would suffer heavy damage should a fight break out. All in all, the saloon looked far better furnished and equipped than one might expect in such a small town. Shipping in the good-quality gear ran to money. Replacing the long bar mirror and the fancy crystal chandelier would be very expensive. So Towcester had no desire to see the start of a range war in his place.

Like his saloon, Towcester seemed more suited to a Kansas trail-end town or prosperous gold camp than a Texas range hamlet—and San Garcia, despite its citizens' claims, was no more than that. Tall, handsome, wearing the cutaway coat, frilly shirt, string tie, fancy vest, tight-legged pants, and town boots of a successful professional gambler, Towcester watched the confrontation of the two ranchers and took action to halt the trouble.

"Stevie!" he hissed to the girl at his side. "Get circulating, pronto!"

Stevie Cameron was another who hardly fitted into the accepted pattern of a small-town saloon. Raven black hair piled gracefully on top of her head, she was the youngest, best-looking girl present. Her blue satin dress emphasized the rich swell of a well-developed bosom, clung to her slender waist, and curved out alluringly over the hips, ending at knee level to expose shapely legs in black silk stockings. Moving from the bar, she signaled to the other girls, and they converged on the Rocking Rafter contingent. All four cowhands suddenly found themselves with a lapful of girl each, and Stevie went to take hold of the rancher's left arm.

"Buy a girl a drink, Cal?" she asked.

"Later, Stevie," Mobstell replied, not taking his eyes from Cordova.

"Then how about you buying me one, Cisco?" the girl went on, releasing Mobstell's arm and walking toward the Mexican.

"Nothing would give me greater pleasure, *chiquita*," Cordova replied. "But at some other time."

However, the presence of Stevie and the other girls lessened the danger of a flare-up between the men. Taking his chance, Towcester went to Corlin's side. The land agent mopped his face with a large red handkerchief. At any time he perspired easily and never more than when involved in a potentially dangerous situation.

"That was close," Corlin breathed.

"Too close," Towcester replied. "You'd best get down to the plaza—"

"It's too early—"

"I don't give a damn! If you go, they'll follow. That way any trouble that comes isn't going to blow up in my place."

"But outside—"

"There'll be women and kids around, and not just those calico cats of mine. I don't reckon either Mobstell or Cordova'll start fuss if there's a chance of women or kids getting hurt."

"I'll go then," Corlin said, darting a glance at the saloon's clock. Mobstell appeared to have called the time wrong on the land agent's appearance, for the fingers read only a quarter to noon. "All right, gents," he called. "Looks like young McGraw's not going to come. Let's go start the sale."

As Corlin left the saloon, the two ranchers followed him. Keeping to opposite sides of the street, their men at their heels, Mobstell and Cordova crossed the plaza. Already most of the town's population had assembled, all eyes on the front of the building that housed the jail and the sheriff's and town marshal's offices. A table stood on the porch before the building, with a bung starter borrowed from the saloon waiting to do service as an auctioneer's mallet. The sheriff came from the office, having made the trip down from the county seat for the occasion. Following him and dwarfing him, Town Marshal Sash Tenby ambled into view. Although holding down the combined post of deputy sheriff and town marshal, Tenby was not an energetic or efficient peace officer. In fact, he held his official positions through his one virtue: He came cheap, an important factor in the eyes of the town's taxpaying citizens. He kept the peace, which entailed little more than tossing a few drunken cowhands or vaqueros in jail one night and releasing them after payment of a fine the following morning, with as little effort as possible. Hoisting up his gun belt on a barrel-sized belly, Tenby crossed to the hitching rail and assumed his second favorite position, sitting on the creaking horizontal pole; given first choice, he would rather have stayed lying on the office's comfortable and well-used couch.

"All right, folks," called Corlin. "We all know why we're here and what's for sale. So I won't waste time talking about it. Can I hear the bidding open?"

From his place, Tenby swept sleepy eyes around the crowd. Being interested in the sale, he overlooked the four-horse wagon that had come to a halt back along the main street. A seventeen-hand paint stallion and a claybank almost as big stood by the wagon, but its occupants had already joined the crowd. Tenby did see two of Seth McGraw's crew in the forefront of the assembled people. Lean, leathery, bearded, dressed as usual in grease-blackened buckskins, Cactus Jones cradled his battered Colt revolving rifle across one arm and darted interested glances about him as if wondering who his next employer might be. Shorter, wiry as a winter-starved bobcat, Horatio Charles Wilberforce, known as Rache, studied Corlin and seemed to be debating whether to blow the land agent's ears off with the wicked eight-gauge twin-barreled shotgun he carried.

"Five hundred dollars!" barked Mobstell, drawing Tenby's attention to him.

"And fifty," Cordova spoke up from another part of the crowd, and the people between the two ranchers began to edge away.

"Six hundred!" Mobstell said.

"And fifty," Cordova said.

"Three thousand!"

Instead of the next bid coming from Mobstell, a third party had taken a hand. A sudden silence came down. Neither Mobstell nor Cordova spoke for a moment, being taken aback by the new element introduced into what they regarded as a matter to be settled between them. Of course, $3,000 would be a reasonable price for the McGraw spread, and neither of them expected to get it for less; but the $2,350 jump in the bidding made them both stop to think. They also looked hard at the man who made it.

Realizing that a third player had taken cards in the game, those people standing closer to the bidder drew away and left him standing isolated in full view of the two ranchers. Six feet tall, lean, dressed in range clothes of expensive cut—although they probably never felt the touch of cattle-raised dust—the man wore a brace of pearl-handled Army Colts in tied-down holsters. His face bore a challenging smile and an expression that hinted that he felt confident of emerging a winner in anything he put his hand to. No cattleman, to eyes that knew the West he spelled *pistolero valiente,* a good one, fast, deadly and as dangerous as a stick-teased diamondback rattlesnake. Not the kind of man one would expect to be making bids on a small ranch, yet he undoubtedly had just done so.

"Three thousand is the bid, gentlemen," Corlin said, sweat glistening on his face. "Do I hear three thousand and fifty?"

Mobstell darted a glance at Cordova, reading the same indecision he himself felt. On hearing the bet and seeing the kind of man making it, Cordova first thought that Mobstell had hired him to bring an unsuspected element into the bidding. Yet the bulky rancher, noted for his ability as a poker player, showed too much surprise and confusion for the expressions to be assumed. Clearly the newcomer was as much a surprise to Mobstell as to Cordova.

"Three thousand, going once," intoned Corlin.

Still the mocking challenge played on the newcomer's face. *Go ahead, up the bidding,* his expression seemed to say to the two ranchers. *I can top any bet you make and call finish to 'em with lead if I have to.*

"Going twice!" Corlin called, reaching for the bung starter.

"Time wants five minutes for noon, mister," a voice from the rear of the crowd announced. "You're in a tolerable hurry to start selling my ranch."

Turning, the crowd looked in the direction of the latest entrant to the already growing dramatic qualities of the situation. Two young men and a very pretty young woman stood at the edge of the plaza. Hat thrust back to show off a fiery red mop of hair, the taller man looked straight at Corlin. The small, insignificant-looking cowhand at the other side of the girl studied the crowd—or certain parts of it—with the same interest those already assembled gave to his companions.

"That must be young Sandy McGraw!" one of the crowd

said in a carrying voice. "I mind him from when he come visiting ole Seth afore the war."

"And me," another citizen continued. "There's no mistaking that head of hair, is there?"

"Damn it, Cousin Dusty," the irrepressible Red Blaze muttered from the corner of his mouth and over Betty Hardin's head, "I'm better-looking than Sandy and I'll surely raise lumps on the fat jasper's pumpkin head if he talks about my hair that ways again."

Restraining a grin, Dusty watched the three bidders for some sign of their reactions to the arrival of "Sandy McGraw." That Red's announcement at such a late moment had aroused comment and created a sensation did not surprise Dusty. In fact, he had counted on it when making his plans. Instead of arriving a day earlier and establishing ownership, Dusty decided they would keep out of sight and make an appearance as late as possible. That way they could learn who wanted to buy the ranch and might shock somebody into making a wrong move.

Both local ranchers showed baffled annoyance, mingled with maybe a touch of relief, as they realized what the presence of "Sandy McGraw" meant. Only the third bidder seemed unaffected. Pulling a silver watch from his vest pocket, he turned his attention back to Corlin.

"I make the time five past twelve," the man announced, without looking at his watch's face. "Make the sale."

"You'd best check the time again," Dusty said. "The money for the back taxes is here, it's five *to* twelve, and so you can't sell."

Slowly the *pistolero* turned, his watch still in hand. "That sounds almost like you're calling me a liar," he said, and the crowd scattered to leave wide, clear space between him and Dusty's party.

"It sounds to me like you're trying to make the time pass too fast," Dusty replied.

"Now hold hard there," Sheriff Washbourne said, stepping forward. "If that young feller is Sandy McGraw, he's entitled to pay the back taxes until noon."

"Why, sure, Sheriff," the hired killer answered.

"And that clock in the office says five to twelve, no matter what your'n gives, mister."

"If that's how you want it, Sheriff," the killer grunted. "All they have to do is walk up here and pay."

"We're aiming to do just that," Dusty replied.

"You doing the talking for McGraw?" asked the killer.

"Why, sure," Dusty answered. "Somebody hired you to speak for them. Sandy's only just got married, so let's say he hired me to speak for him."

"All right then," said the killer. "Come ahead. All you have to do is pass me."

"Hold hard there—" began Washbourne.

"The name's Damon, Sheriff," the killer said. "That short-growed runt as good as called me a liar. You reckon I'm going to let him get away with that."

Washbourne did not reply for a moment. He was no coward, but folly also did not number among his failings. A capable peace officer, he kept in touch with the happenings in the neighboring counties and knew the man called Damon's reputation. Appearances did not lie. Damon was a *pistolero valiente* and good with a gun. Certainly far better than the sheriff. Before Washbourne could decide what his best course of action might be, Dusty took the matter out of his hands.

"I aim to walk up there and pay Sandy's back taxes, mister," he said, and moved forward.

"You've got another four steps, short-growed," Damon replied, and started to put away his watch.

Suddenly the killer realized that he faced the real thing, not merely some small youngster trying to make a grandstand play in a big man's world. That gun belt hung just right for top speed work, and the *big* cowhand walking toward him could make full use of its potential. However, Damon knew a trick or two and had already begun to make his move.

Even as he dropped the watch back into the vest pocket, Damon sent his left hand gunward. Fast and practiced, the move also had the element of complete surprise to back it. Although a number of men wore two guns, only a few learned to use each hand with equal facility. Nor did the majority of people take the left hand into consideration, especially when the man in question appeared to follow the general trend by being right-handed. So reaching with his left hand always gave Damon a split second's advantage.

Always—until he made the move against Dusty Fog.

Having trained himself to be completely ambidextrous, partly as a way of taking attention as a child from his lack of size, Dusty never discounted the left hand when dealing with a two-gun man. For all that, the move proved nearly good enough. Only by a slight flicker of expression did Damon give warning of his intentions. Certain that he had the other man completely hornswoggled, the killer allowed the fact to show momentarily.

So Dusty's own left hand moved to counter the threat to his life. Having flicked across his body, the hand closed about the butt of the right-side Colt and brought it from leather. Damon's face showed the start of a feeling of shock and surprise when a .44-caliber bullet drove between his eyes and wiped out all its expression. Only just clear of leather, his gun bellowed, and its bullet churned dirt up scant inches in front of Dusty's foot as it came down for the second step since Damon gave the warning. Limp, lifeless fingers opened to let Damon's revolver fall from them. The killer went backward under the impact, and he sprawled onto the street. Halting, Dusty looked down, smoke trickling out of his Colt's muzzle.

"Go pay the man, Sandy," he said. "There's still time."

10

Nobody spoke or moved as Red and Betty walked along the open path left by the crowd, passing Dusty as they went toward the waiting group on the porch. Tenby now stood up, staring at Damon's body as if unable to believe the evidence of his eyes. Pale, face running sweat, Corlin darted glances around him as if in search of advice on what to do. Not that he had any great choice in the matter, with the fingers of the office clock still not having come together over the figures twelve.

Holstering his Colt, Dusty looked around the crowd, searching for some sign of disappointment at Damon's failure to hold off the payment of the back taxes. He saw nothing that helped and so followed his cousins onto the porch. Mopping his face, Corlin studied Red, then directed a worried glance in Dusty's direction. The land agent's whole attitude was that of a man with an unpleasant and possibly dangerous task ahead of him.

"I—I suppose that you can produce proof of your identity,

Mr. McGraw," he said, darting a worried glance in the marshal's direction as if seeking protection.

"Just how'd you mean, proof?" asked Red.

"In view of the value of the property and the fact that I've heard nothing from you—" Corlin began.

"I wrote and told you that I'd be coming," Red interrupted.

"But I never received any letter!" Corlin protested. "That's why I arranged the sale. However, under the circumstances I think we can put that aside. If you offer me satisfactory proof of your identity, I will accept your payment."

"I know Sandy McGraw pretty well," Dusty pointed out.

Corlin gulped and jerked his head in Dusty's direction. Any man so fast with a gun possessed a mighty convincing argument in his favor. If he made an issue of having his word accepted, neither the sheriff nor the marshal could lick his draw in defense of the land agent.

"Th-that's hardly what I meant," Corlin finally croaked.

"Maybe these'll help," Red drawled, pulling four letters from his pocket and offering them to the agent.

Without taking it, Corlin recognized the top envelope. On accepting the offered evidence, he drew out his own letter telling Sandy of the back taxes and setting the date for payment, also warning of the forfeit should it not be made on time. The second letter had been sent by Moses Birnbaum, local lawyer currently on a visit to El Paso. It informed Sandy of his uncle's death and that Seth had left him the ranch. Drawing out the third letter, Corlin found it to be from Marshal Anse Dale of San Antonio and to introduce its bearer as Rufus Hamish McGraw, known as Sandy. Lastly Corlin studied a similar letter of introduction signed by Dustine Edward Marsden Fog for General O. D. Hardin.

"Satisfied?" asked Red.

While the evidence certainly appeared satisfactory, Corlin could think of an unpleasant explanation of how they had come into the redhead's hands. However, the land agent felt sure that any suggestion of the newcomers' having come by the letters dishonestly would not be kindly received. An interruption came to save Corlin from reaching a decision. Having moved

up unnoticed and listened to the conversation, Cactus and
Rache swung themselves onto the porch.

"Well, I swan!" Cactus boomed. "If young Sandy ain't done
forgot his ole Uncle Cactus and Uncle Rache."

"Waal, he ain't seed us since afore the war," Rache pointed
out.

"You recognize him then?" asked Corlin.

"He's a mite older'n when we saw him last, afore the war,"
Cactus replied. "Looks like his pappy, though. Why, Sam 'n'
Bertha McGraw must've been real proud of you, boy, when
they heard you was a sergeant in General Hood's Texas Bri-
gade."

"They sure would've been, only their names were Mavis-
Belle and Hamish," Red replied. "And I never even made cor-
poral. Best I got was carrying the company guidon for Cap'n
Dusty Fog."

"Cactus's getting old, boy," Rache said by way of apology.
"Couldn't even remember what Seth claimed he used to call
you when you was a sprout, and neither could I."

"Then even if I tell you it was Hoppy on account of me
hopping all 'round the place, you won't know any difference."
Red grinned.

"Danged effen he's not right, Rache," Cactus declared, slapping his thigh with the hand not holding the rifle. "Looks like
we've done met up with our new boss. Allus figuring he wants a
couple of ole no-accounts like us around."

"Like Uncle Seth always said," Red replied, "I may as well
hire you pair. You don't eat as much and come cheaper than
one good hand."

Despite the way in which the two old-timers accepted Red,
Dusty felt sure something was wrong. Before leaving San Antonio, the three cousins had learned as much as possible from
Sandy's past. They had collected many apparently unimportant
details, little things that one would expect only the genuine
person to know. At the back of Dusty's mind, a half-recalled
memory fought to gain recognition and failed.

"You got a minute to spare, friend?" asked the sheriff, coming to Dusty's side while Red gave Corlin his attention.

"Why, sure," Dusty answered.

No matter how Dusty felt, it seemed that Corlin accepted Red's bona fides. Taking the money Red offered, the land agent started the formalities to make Sandy McGraw legal owner of the Lazy M ranch. Dusty and the sheriff walked along the porch and, although watched by some of the crowd, halted where their voices would not reach other ears.

"I'd say you've used a gun afore today," Washbourne remarked, nodding to where people gathered about Damon's body. "Fact being there's not many around can handle one that good."

"Thanks," Dusty replied.

"I'm being polite and hinting to learn your name," Washbourne stated.

"And if I don't feel like telling you it?" asked Dusty.

"I'm not fast enough to make you tell me," admitted the sheriff. "But I'll just have to make a stab at it."

"The sheriff down to Rio Hondo County allowed you're just about stubborn enough to try it."

"This sheriff down there. You know him real good?"

"I should," Dusty said. "He's my father. Only I'd as soon nobody knew about it just yet."

"It's a sinful shame when a man's ashamed of his own kin, not that I blame you in this case." Washbourne grinned, pleased that his guess at the small Texan's identity turned out to be a meat-in-the-pot hit. "What's it all about, Mr.—Smith?"

"Make it Jones, Sheriff," Dusty said. "I'm a snob. What do you know about that jasper I killed?"

"He's a *pistolero valiente,* which you already know."

"Work around here?"

"Not as I know about," Washbourne replied. "Mind you, though, I don't come up this way more than three, four times a year, but I get around to hearing most that happens."

"From that real smart-looking deputy there?" asked Dusty, nodding to where Tenby made a lethargic way toward the body.

"He's cheap—and folks watch him instead of the feller who

lets me know about things," the sheriff answered. "I figure it's time you answered some of *my* questions now."

"That's easy," Dusty said. "Sandy McGraw rode with my company in the war. Asked me down to San Antonio for his wedding. When somebody tried to kill both him and his wife the night before the wedding, I allowed he might need help."

"That sort of thing does make you feel thataways," Washbourne drawled. "You know who wanted to kill Sandy?"

"A hired gun called Paco Murphy."

"Name means nothing to me," Washbourne confessed. "Not that that counts for anything, way his sort change their names."

Even when Dusty described Murphy, the sheriff still continued to disclaim all knowledge of the man. However, Washbourne promised that he would make inquiries both from his local informant and at the county seat. Then he and Dusty turned back to see how Red was faring with the land agent.

Although some of the people came to greet and introduce themselves to the "McGraws," both ranchers walked away without speaking. Seeing that there would be no further dramatic developments, the crowd started to disperse. Cordova and his men rode out of town, but the Rocking Rafter cowhands returned to the Golden Goose saloon while their boss went to attend to some business.

"You folks coming right out to the ranch?" Cactus asked as Dusty rejoined his cousins.

"We've a few things to do around town first," Red replied.

"Why not take your hosses into the livery barn while you're waiting then?" Rache suggested.

"It'd be best," Dusty answered. "Let's do just that."

Glancing to where the sheriff had joined the town marshal, Dusty saw them look his way. It seemed that Washbourne satisfied Tenby's curiosity, for the marshal did not bother to ask Dusty any questions. Instead he went off after four men who were carrying Damon's body to the undertaker's premises. Most of the crowd had gone, and those who had stayed to speak with Betty and Red moved away. At the table Corlin looked down at a receipt Red had signed for the title deeds to the ranch. Then the land agent stared harder, opened his mouth as if to say something, thought better of it, and remained silent. He stared hard at Red for a time before folding up the receipt and dropping it into his pocket.

Followed by the two old-timers, Dusty, Betty, and Red returned to the wagon. On reaching the livery stable, they found it deserted and prepared to care for their horses themselves. After unbuckling the double girths, Dusty gripped the horn and cantle of his saddle ready to remove it.

"Just sorta keep your hands there, young feller," Cactus said.

Looking over his shoulder, without moving his hands, Dusty gazed into the .56-caliber bore of the Colt revolving rifle. More than that, Rache's shotgun lingered negligently, casually, but directly on Red's back as he, too, stood with hands on his saddle.

"Something bothering you?" Red asked.

"Waal, now, that's a real good question," Cactus answered. "Thing bothering me is who you be."

"Sandy McGraw, most folks'd say," Red drawled.

"Know plenty about him, too," said Rache. "Only you made one lil mistake in it."

"Mind how you met us here afore the war?" asked Cactus mildly.

"Sure," Red replied.

"Only we warn't here afore the war," Cactus stated. "We was—"

"Running contraband down on the border," Dusty finished for him, the half-remembered fact leaping into focus.

For a moment the rifle wavered, and Cactus came as near to showing surprise as ever in his life. "Now how'd you know that?"

"I've heard the Ysabel Kid talk about you," Dusty explained.

"Do you think I'm going to need this, Dusty?" Betty asked, making a small gesture with the Remington double derringer she had drawn at the first sign of trouble.

"How long you been pointing that thing at us, ma'am?" Rache inquired, letting his shotgun's muzzle sag a trifle.

"Long enough to figure I won't have to use it." Betty smiled.

"Reckon you could hit us with that itty-bitty stingy gun, ma'am?" Cactus went on, returning the rifle to across the crook of his elbow.

"You'd better believe it," Betty replied. "Or you could ask the Ysabel Kid."

"Is Cuchilo hereabouts then?" asked Cactus, using the Kid's Indian name.

"Not right now," Dusty replied. "And I'm going to take this saddle off before my hoss kicks my feet from under me."

"Now lookee here," protested Rache, "we's all sociable and getting on like the deacon to firewater. But I allows somebody should ought to tell us where young Sandy be."

After swinging his saddle from the paint, Dusty carried it to the wooden rack at the side of the barn. Then he told the old-timers of the incidents that brought himself and his cousins to San Garcia instead of Sandy and Sarah McGraw. An angry growl rumbled in Cactus's throat on hearing of Sandy's accident, and Rache cut loose with a curse, remembered Betty's presence, and apologized with another for his previous profanity.

"Figure we owe you-all a forgiveness," Cactus said, silencing his companion by jerking his battered Stetson over his eyes. "We knowed you wasn't young Sandy, mister, but you knew stuff he'd only tell a friend. So we didn't let on in front of the folks."

"Why make with all the high drama then?" asked Red, placing his saddle by Dusty's. "Pointing those rusted-up ole relics and all."

"We're jest a couple of wored-out, useless ole goats—" Cactus began.

"*You* said it," Red pointed out.

"Like I was saying"—the old-timer sniffed—"we ain't smart like you young sprouts's has had book l'arning—"

"But we're long on low cunning," interrupted Rache. "And afore you says it, I just now said it."

"Like Horatio here done stated, we-all long on low cunning," said Cactus. "So we figures that you not being Sandy, you mightn't go for folks mentioning it to you."

"Which same we figures also that the time to start asking about it's after you boys warn't in no position to argufy the point," Rache continued. "Only when we was young, a well-raised young lady didn't go pointing no gun at folks old enough to be her grandpappy."

"Now you knowing the Kid so well raises a smart point," Cactus remarked. "I mind a name you hear spoke a lot along of the Kid's. You wouldn't be—"

"This's my cousin Edward Marsden," Betty put in.

"Right pleased to know you, Mr. Marsden." Cactus grinned. "Did anybody ever tell you how much you look like Cap'n Dusty Fog?"

"He's fatter and not so good-looking as Cousin Ed." Red grinned back. "Folks do say I feature that handsome, charming, witty, dashing young Red Blaze, though."

"And you'd be Mrs. Blaze, ma'am?" asked Rache.

"Not for any price!" Betty snorted.

"Sandy having just got married, we figured I'd be accepted better if I had a wife along," Red explained. "My wife Sue's back home, so I offered to go out and find a right pretty lil gal to come along. Couldn't find one, so I brought her instead."

"You wouldn't want me to tell that story to Sue when we get home, now would you, cousin, dear?" Betty purred.

Friendly relations had been reestablished, and the cousins did not blame the old-timers for taking precautions. Dusty brought the conversation to a more serious level and described Murphy, asking if either of the old men knew him.

"I'd swear he's not been around here," Cactus stated.

"Who'd want the ranch bad enough to hire Murphy and send him after Sandy?" asked Dusty.

"Nobody I can think of," Cactus replied, and Rache nodded agreement.

"How about those two ranchers who were bidding to buy the spread?"

"Cal Mobstell only wanted it to stop Cisco Cordova getting

it, Cap'n," the bearded oldster answered. "And the same applies the other way about."

"Then where's that gunslick fit in?" Red asked. "He for sure wanted to buy."

"Might've just been looking for some place to settle down and make a home," Rache suggested. "Figured on hanging up his guns and making a living ranching."

"Forcing the other bidders out'd be a swell way of doing that," Dusty said. "Nope. There's another reason for him coming here and joining the bidding. There has to be."

"Could be he works for one of those big Yankee companies that're buying into the cattle business now we've got it bringing in profit," Betty remarked. "Some of them aren't choosy how they gain control."

"Would they want a small spread like the Lazy M?" Red asked.

"It'd be a start," Dusty answered. "What sort of spread is it, Cactus? I mean, does it control the water hereabouts?"

"Nope. We got our share of water, but so've the Rocking Rafter and Whangdoodle. Even if we wanted to, we couldn't dry them out."

"How'd Seth die?"

"Just took sick and went, Cap'n."

"At the ranch?"

"Nope," replied Cactus. "Here in town."

"We'd come in to spend our pay, and he took sick down at the Golden Goose," Rache added. "He'd gone afore the doctor got to him."

"Did the doctor say what he thought caused him to die?" Dusty inquired.

"Allowed it war appendi something or such," answered Rache, his tone showing that he placed little faith in the doctor's ability. "Ole Seth got this pain in his guts—that's Kiowa for stomach, ma'am—and doubled over like he'd been kicked by a knobhead.* We got him up to Miss Stevie's room, but

* Knobhead: a mule.

Towcester, him being the new boss at the Golden Goose, would have that fancy dude doctor come see him."

"I told them all Seth needed was a good dosing with croton oil," Cactus stated. "All them newfangled medical notions are good for neither men nor beast."

"Had anybody showed any interest in buying the ranch, either before or after Seth died?" Dusty asked, making a mental note to question the doctor at the first opportunity.

"Anybody's knowed Seth'd not waste his time. You couldn't've bought the Lazy M with the whole damned First National Bank's money, way he felt about the place."

"Rache's never said a truer word," said Cactus. "And nobody's said anything to us since he died."

"Anybody been coming around like they were looking it over?" Dusty said, deciding that an early visit to the lawyer who handled McGraw's will was also called for.

"Not that we've seen," admitted Cactus, but Rache disagreed.

"Two or three times I've seen Towcester and Miss Stevie out there."

"What were they doing?" asked Red.

"And you a married man, for shame." Cactus sniffed. "I'd say he was doing the same as you used to do when you took your good lady buggy riding when you was sparking her."

"The dirty dog." Red grinned.

"Danged if we ain't getting old, Cactus," growled Rache, slapping a hand on his thigh. "How's about that lard-gutted marshal?"

"What about him?" demanded Dusty.

"We've come across him two, three times riding the range and allowing to be hunting for owlhoots."

"And was he?"

"Tell you, Cap'n," Rache replied, "I'd sooner say no to that. He may've been a fair miner one time, but he's no great shucks as a peace officer."

"A miner?" Dusty repeated.

"Waal, he's never told us so," Rache admitted, "but he uses a

slew of miner talk; you know, like a cowhand talks cattle. I'd
say Tenby's spent plenty time in mining camps."

"Could he be doing some prospecting hereabouts on the
side?" Red said.

"He's picked the wrong sort of country if he is," Rache replied. "I was out to Californy in '49 and done my share of gold
hunting. First time I heard Tenby'd been seed owlhoot hunting,
I took out and searched the high country. Unless I'm plenty
mistooked, there's no gold in them there hills."

While talking, the men saw to their horses' needs. After un-
saddling their mounts, Red and Dusty put them into stalls.
Betty tended to her roan, which had been brought along roped
at the rear of the wagon. Helped by the two now-willing old-
timers, Dusty and Red unhitched the wagon's team. As they
finished off the feeding and watering, Dusty learned about local
conditions. Apart from the usual interranch rivalry there was
no hostility between the local spreads. Neither Mobstell nor
Cordova had shown any interest in occupying the Lazy M during Seth's lifetime and, in fact, tended to regard it as a buffer
state between their outfits. Reserving his judgment until after
he met the two ranchers, Dusty brought the meeting to a close.

"We're going to stay in town a spell, Cactus," he said. "How
about you?"

"I reckon we'll ride back and tell the others that they've still
got a home, Cap'n," the old-timer replied. "And after that
Damon *hombre* showing up, I'll have the boys keep their eyes
open real careful."

"That'd maybe be best," Dusty said. "I've a feeling this business goes a whole heap deeper than we know."

11

Dusty had decided to visit the local doctor. From what the two old-timers told him about the doctor, Dusty concluded that he might expect answers to his questions only if accompanied by somebody of local importance and official standing. Catching the sheriff on the verge of returning to the county seat, Dusty explained what he wanted, and together they went to the doctor's house.

Dr. Hugo Paczek was a slim young man with an air of constantly being in a hurry. Cultivated during his time in medical school, the air made most people believe him to be waiting to set about some urgent business of saving a life. Standing at his desk—he always interviewed people on his feet as a further aid to his pose—the doctor looked at Dusty and the sheriff.

"I'm expected on a house call, gentlemen," he stated.

"This won't take long, Doc," Washbourne replied. "We want to know a few things about Seth McGraw."

"How'd you mean?"

"Cap'n—Marsden here's been asking me about it."

"Captain?" Paczek repeated, eyeing Dusty in a disbelieving manner.

"You've heard of the Texas Rangers, I reckon," Washbourne answered.

"Of course," Paczek agreed, and studied Dusty with fresh interest.

Everybody in the Lone Star State knew that the Texas Rangers had been reorganized to replace the disbanded Davis government's state police. Unlike their inefficient, unlamented predecessors, the Rangers wore no uniform and kept their badges of office hidden until needed. Maybe that small man looked like a nobody, but a captain in the Texas Rangers packed a whole heap of weight in the state.

"What do you want to know, Captain?" Paczek inquired politely.

"How did Seth die?"

"Of acute appendicitis."

"What'd that be, Doc?" Washbourne asked.

"An inflammation of that part of the large intestine called the appendix," Paczek replied.

"Have you seen many cases of it, Doctor?" Dusty said.

"Er—a few."

"Did the folks you saw die from it?"

"Some did. The damage can be repaired by removal of the appendix, but it is a serious, dangerous operation."

"You'd know how to do that operation?"

"I'd know, but I wouldn't want to chance it," Paczek replied cautiously. "In this case the need did not arise. By the time I saw him, Mr. McGraw was too far gone for me to save him."

"You knew that he'd got this appendicitis, though?" Dusty continued.

"Of course. All the symptoms were there."

"Do they show real plain?"

Watching Dusty question Paczek, Washbourne felt his conscience ease. Maybe Captain Fog had no official connection with the Texas Rangers, but he sure knew a peace officer's work. Certainly Paczek did not suspect that the sheriff had evaded his unasked question concerning Dusty's position and right to ask about McGraw's death, although he looked a mite impatient.

"Plain enough," the doctor answered. "It begins with pain in the upper abdomen, and then the pain sinks to the right lower quadrant of the abdomen. There is nausea and later vomiting, excessive perspiration. Until the appendix ruptures—bursts, that is—the patient has a fifty-fifty chance of recovery if he can be operated on in time. Unfortunately by the time I arrived the rupture had occurred, and McGraw died before I could do anything."

"How'd you know about the pains and the rest, Doctor?" Dusty wanted to know. "They wouldn't show that late, or would they?"

"Usually the patient can describe them—"

"Only this time he couldn't."

"No, Captain. However, Mr. Towcester at the saloon described them. You see, I'd been out of town attending a confinement, and when the news reached me, I could not leave the mother. When I did arrive at the saloon, it was too late for me to question McGraw. Mr. Towcester told me how McGraw complained of the pains and was sick at least once during the evening, then collapsed."

"How'd man get this appendicitis, Doctor?" Dusty asked. "I mean, can he catch it like typhoid?"

"Certainly not. The most probable cause is an obstruction to the normal emptying of the appendix."

"And there's no way it can be made to happen, deliberately, I mean?"

"Not that I know of," said Paczek, then realized what the question implied. "You don't think that Mr. McGraw was murdered?"

"Somebody tried to kill Mr. and Mrs. McGraw in San Antonio, Doctor," Dusty replied, watching Paczek's face. "So it started me wondering how his uncle died—"

"It's all in the coroner's report," Paczek answered.

"You opened him up to make sure it was appendicitis, Doctor?" Washbourne asked.

"Well, I—" Paczek began. Then indignation glowed on his face. "Sheriff, I'm the only doctor at this end of the county. There's always enough work to do on the living without—"

"You didn't open the body then, Doctor?" Dusty interrupted.

"I was too busy!" Paczek snapped. "There was that mother and baby, and a cowhand at the Rocking Rafter was gored by a bull. You know that in the heat we had at that time we had to bury the body quickly. Everything pointed clearly to a case of acute appendicitis, so why should I—"

"Take it easy, Doctor," Dusty said gently. "As long as you're sure he died of natural causes, that's all we need to know."

"I'm sure!" Paczek stated, maybe just a shade too confidently.

"Then we don't need to take up any more of your valuable time," Dusty told him. "I'd be right obliged if you kept this visit to yourself, Doctor."

"You can rely on me for that!" Paczek assured him.

Outside the doctor's home Washbourne looked at Dusty. "Damn it, Dusty! He wasn't sure at all."

"Nope," Dusty said. "But a feller like him would bust a gut before he'd admit that to a couple of uneducated jaspers like us."

"If he was wrong—" growled the sheriff.

"It starts a man thinking, doesn't it?" Dusty drawled. "I reckon I'll look in at the saloon. What do you know about the feller who runs it?"

"Not much. He bought it maybe six months back. Fixed it up real good, runs it dead fair. I've had no complaints about him or the place. Do you want for me to come with you?"

"This's one time when I don't want official backing." Dusty smiled. "I reckon that Red and I can learn more that way. How'd I reach you if I have to?"

"See Frenchy Becque at the Wells Fargo office; he'll let me know."

After the sheriff left, Dusty made his way to the general store. There he found a bored Red idly examining a Winchester rifle, while Betty stood in the center of a group of local women. Laying aside the rifle, Red joined Dusty and showed no reluctance to visit the saloon. So they interrupted the women, told Betty that they had business to attend to along the street, and left the store.

Entering the saloon, the cousins paused just inside and looked around them with considerable interest. Having seen such places in a variety of towns, Dusty and Red could estimate the upkeep and cost of the Golden Goose's fittings. They exchanged glances as each reached the same conclusion. A saloon of that quality did not belong in a small range town.

Across the room Mobstell's four hands sat moodily glaring at the glasses of beer that were all their finances ran to. With no danger of trouble, the girls no longer offered to entertain the quartet, giving attention to the other customers in the room.

"How's about having a drink, Stevie?" asked Bob Lynn as the girl approached his table.

"Not right now," she replied. "Beer's bad for my complexion."

An angry scowl creased Lynn's face, for he had spent the majority of his last month's pay entertaining Stevie. Not a badlooking young man, he fancied himself as something of a ladykiller, and the girl's indifference annoyed him. Nor did his feelings improve when he saw Stevie make for Dusty and Red.

"If you're thinking what I think you're thinking, forget it," Stevie told Red with a smile as he looked up at the chandelier. "The last three men who tried to bust it went out here on a shutter."

"The thought never entered my head, ma'am." Red grinned, removing his hat and looking the girl over with interest.

"You're new here, aren't you?" Stevie inquired.

"Just now got in. I'm—"

"Sandy McGraw, the new owner of the Lazy M," Stevie interrupted. "And you are—"

"Marsden's the name, ma'am," Dusty answered. "Ed Marsden. Sandy and me rode in the same outfit through the war."

"I'm Stevie Cameron," the girl said. "Come across to the bar. You must meet the boss."

"You'll have a drink with us, ma'am?" Red asked as the girl walked with them by the four cowhands' table.

"It'd be a pleasure." Stevie smiled back. "Wine, if that's possible?"

"If they've got it, it's yours, ma'am," Red assured her.

However, Towcester insisted on standing the first round of drinks on the house. Red warned that he would not be staying long, because of having his wife waiting to go out to their new home, but Towcester laughed it off.

"This's a real nice place you have here," Dusty commented, looking around.

"I always wanted my own place," Towcester replied. "And I figured that if I was setting up, I ought to do it right."

"You've sure done that," Dusty said, glancing at the fittings.

"It pays. Fellers come here instead of the county seat on paydays. That way San Garcia draws more trade. Why, I wouldn't be surprised if one day we don't take over as county seat."

Knowing cowhands, Dusty decided that they would be willing to ride the extra few miles to drink in such a fancy saloon. He could also see how the town benefited by the Golden Goose's presence. Studying Towcester, Dusty concluded that he was a shrewd businessman likely to keep both eyes on the profit and loss columns of his books. However, before Dusty could make a start at learning about Seth McGraw's illness, an interruption came.

At his table Bob Lynn scowled at the cousins as they stood talking with Stevie and Towcester. When the girl laughed at something Red said, Lynn started to rise. Shooting a hand out, Avon caught his companion's arm and held him in the chair.

"Easy there, Bob," he warned. "That gunslick'd blow your ears off starting in the middle."

"That's for sure," Shanty said.

"There's a way 'round it," Lynn growled, dropping his hands to his belt buckle. "We'll soon show Stevie what that pair's like."

Hearing his plan, the other three admitted it possessed a number of virtues and offered to help put it into action. After making certain adjustments to their dress, they rose and walked toward the bar.

"Yes, Miss Stevie," Red was saying. "I'm sure looking forward to living here in San Garcia."

"So you're Sandy McGraw," Lynn interrupted. "Waal, I'm Bob Lynn."

"Now we know each other," Red replied.

"We've knowed each other a fair whiles," Lynn informed him. "Fact being, the last time we was here, I tossed you into Tres Manos Creek."

"Ole Bob sure licked you good that time," Shanty went on. "Course, you didn't have that gunslick backing you then."

Suddenly the cousins realized that none of the four cowhands wore a gun. Dusty felt sure that he would have noticed during his study of the quartet as they stood behind their boss in the plaza what amounted to a phenomenon in the state of Texas. Looking further, he concluded that the cowhands had been drinking. Not much, but sufficient to make them truculent, quarrelsome, and dangerous. At Dusty's side, a ruddy tint crept into Red's cheeks. Knowing the signs, Dusty prepared for trouble.

"Now me," Red said, "I don't recall getting licked at all."

"Which's just the same as calling Bob a liar," Clayd put in.

"I'd chance doing it, too," Shanty commented, "was I facing a man who ain't heeled and backed by that gunslick."

"That's soon settled," Red stated, and started to unbuckle his belt.

"Your hired gun's still wearing h—" Lynn began.

The words trailed off as Lynn saw that Dusty was also unbuckling his gun belt. Even while doing so, Dusty cursed his luck. Most probably he could prevent a fight if the cowhands knew his true identity, but he wished to keep that a secret for as long as possible. One thing Dusty did know. Red would not backwater, so he must help his cousin and let the cards fall where they would.

"Shall we debate the matter further, Senator?" asked Red, laying his gun belt on the bar and removing his hat.

"I yield to the gent with the real big mouth," Dusty answered, his matched Colts and Stetson joining Red's property on the bar top. "He's put up the bill before the house. Let him make his choice."

"You aiming to fight us?" Shanty inquired. "No guns, tooth 'n' claw?"

"Now me," Dusty replied, "I'd say that was up to you."

"It's a mite uneven," Avon pointed out. "There's four of us and two of you."

"Maybe," Red answered. "But we don't have time to wait for you to get more help."

"Why, you—" Lynn began.

"Just hold it a mite, Bob, boys!" ordered the bartender, producing a sawed-off twin-barreled ten-gauge shotgun from under the counter. "I ain't objecting to you fighting. But on the plaza, not in here."

"Anyways you want it, friend," Dusty said. "Keep your eye on our belts for a spell. It shouldn't take us long."

"I'll see to them like they was my own," promised the bartender.

Chairs scraped back and men rose as the two cousins walked by the Rocking Rafter cowhands and across the room. Followed by the quartet, Dusty and Red passed through the batwing doors and onto the sidewalk. Stepping forward, Lynn linked his fingers and crashed both hands down toward the back of Red's neck. Instinct and a pair of quick ears saved Red from what, in cowhand circles, was a perfectly legal attack. Although he moved forward and avoided the full impact, the blow still staggered him toward the edge of the porch. However, Red retained control of himself. Having hooked an arm around the nearest supporting beam of the porch, Red swung around it, ducked under the hitching rail, and slammed his own fists behind Lynn's neck as the cowhand charged after him. With a yell of mingled surprise, pain, and anger, Lynn shot off the sidewalk and went sprawling to his hands and knees on the street.

Even as Lynn attacked Red, Avon lunged forward and clamped hold of Dusty's neck from behind. Just what he in-

tended to do next nobody ever learned. Most people would
have pulled away from the grip, but Dusty did not. As soon as
he felt the hands touch him, he leaned backward. That had the
effect of easing the grip on him. Up and back whipped Dusty's
hands, closing on Avon's wrists. At the same moment Dusty
used his right foot as a pivot and turned his entire body to the
left. After jerking the hands from his throat, Dusty carried
Avon's right arm upward and drew the left underneath it. By
forcing down the right arm on the left and throwing his own
weight forward, Dusty caused Avon's feet to leave the ground.
The cowhand's body turned a somersault, flew off the sidewalk,
and struck the dirt of the plaza with a satisfying thud. Only the
fact that he possessed considerable ability as a rider of bad
horses saved Avon. Skilled at taking unexpected falls, he landed
with enough force to jolt the wind from his body, but he
avoided injury.

To give them their due, Clayd and Shanty did not intend to
cut into the fight. Removing their gun belts had merely been to
prevent the cousins from using their being armed as an excuse
for not fighting. However, seeing their friends handled in such a
casual, easy manner caused them to change their minds. The
honor of the Rocking Rafter was at stake, and they started
through the batwing doors with the intention of upholding it.

"Dusty!" Red snapped, seeing the danger.

"Give 'em a spin!" Dusty replied, also turning.

Much to Clayd and Shanty's surprise, Dusty darted behind
his cousin instead of at them. In passing, Dusty extended his
left arm, and Red caught his wrist in both hands. Swinging
around, Red heaved at Dusty's arm and lent impetus to his
cousin's speed. Already turning to meet the advancing cowhands, Dusty leaped into the air and drove both feet out. Pow-
ered by Red's heave and his own velocity, Dusty's boots thudded with considerable force into Clayd's and Shanty's chests.
Clayd shot backward through the batwing doors and disappeared into the saloon. Having crashed into the wall alongside
the door, Shanty bounced off and toward trouble. Red released
Dusty's arm as soon as the boots did their work. Around lashed

his left hand, ripping a punch almost wrist-deep into Shanty's advancing belly. An explosive croak burst from the burly cowhand, and he doubled over. Up whipped Dusty's right knee, full into the bearded face that Red's punch conveniently presented for that purpose. Lifted erect again, Shanty once more collided with the wall. For a moment he hung up against the wall, his face a blank mask. Then he slid down to sit motionless on the sidewalk.

Turning after hitting Shanty, Red hurled himself off the sidewalk and landed on Lynn as the other charged into the attack. Wheezing a mite, Avon sat up and looked around, then started to rise. At the same moment a wild-eyed, cursing Clayd burst out of the saloon.

Going under Clayd's flying fists, Dusty butted him in the belly. As the cowhand doubled over, Dusty straightened up and, by catching Clayd around the knees with his hands, pitched him over. Clayd landed on Avon as the other tried to reach the sidewalk, and they went down in a cursing, yelling, tangled pile. Throwing a glance at Shanty, to make sure he would not be interfering for a while, Dusty saw the big man still sitting, shaking his head and looking dazed. Satisfied there would be no danger from that source, Dusty swung around and stepped from the sidewalk. After rolling Clayd from him, Avon rose fast and came for Dusty in a way that showed he knew how to handle himself in a fight.

Already a growing crowd had gathered, the saloon's occupants being augmented by everybody in town who could run, walk, or hobble alóng. While the killing of Damon had provided a reasonable climax to the attempted auction of the Lazy M, San Garcia's citizens had hoped for a more protracted fight. So they gathered fast, forming around the fighters in a figure that constantly altered shape as dictated by the movements of the struggling men. While trading punches with Avon, Dusty caught a glimpse of Betty standing in the forefront of the crowd on the porch. One glance at the expression on her face was all the small Texan needed to know that he and Red would hear more of the matter at a later date.

A pair of arms clamped around Dusty from behind, one circling his neck and the other around his waist without holding his arms. Clearly Clayd had recovered enough to rejoin the proceedings and must be dealt with as fast as possible. Throwing back his head, Dusty cracked the base of his skull hard into Clayd's nose but did not effect a release. Taking his chance, Avon ripped a punch to Dusty's face. Fully occupied with Lynn in giving the crowd as good a fight as San Garcia had ever witnessed, Red could not help his cousin. Not that Dusty waited for help. Up drove his foot, catching Avon in the belly and sending him staggering backward. Then Dusty caught hold of the arm around his throat, dropped to one knee, and flipped Clayd over his shoulder.

Even as Dusty rose, he saw Red coming his way, propelled backward by a punch from Lynn. Bringing his hands up, Dusty halted Red's retreat and thrust him forward. Lynn had been following up on his punch, and the sudden reversal of direction took him by surprise; he walked full into Red's fist and reeled under its impact. Catching his balance, he halted Red's rush with a jab to the mouth and took a hook in his ribs that brought a gasp of pain.

As Dusty started to leap over Clayd's body to get at Avon, he felt the young cowhand catch his left ankle and heave. Having landed on his hands to break his fall, Dusty lashed backward with his free leg, and his boot caught Clayd's already bleeding, throbbing nose, to cause an immediate release of the captured ankle. Seeing his chance, Avon sprang forward and kicked Dusty in the ribs. Pain knifed through the small Texan as he pitched over to land on his back. Following Dusty, Avon tried to drop and ram a knee into his chest. Although Dusty just managed to avoid the crushing impact of the knee, it struck him a glancing blow and slid off him. Before he could make a move, Avon knelt at his side and gripped his throat in both hands. Avon tried to smash Dusty's head against the ground. To the side Clayd rose. Wiping a hand across his face, the youngster stared at the blood on it, let out a snarl, and lurched toward Avon and Dusty.

Unnoticed by Dusty, Shanty had made his feet and pushed through the crowd to halt behind Betty. At the same moment Betty let out an angry hiss and started to go to her cousin's aid. Seeing that, Shanty decided to prevent her from doing so. A grin twisted his bearded face as he hooked his right arm around Betty's waist from behind.

"You keep out o—" he began.

By that time Betty had been given a chance to decide on what course of action she should take. Gripping the big right hand in her right with its thumb in the center of the hairy back and fingers on his palm, she hacked back at his shin with her left boot's heel. While Betty did not wear her spurs, the kick packed enough force to make Shanty relax his crushing pressure. Twisting herself around and away from the man, Betty carried his right hand upward, and the way she held it caused his whole arm to turn so the back of his hand faced the ground. Now Betty stood slightly to Shanty's rear. Swiftly she brought her left hand onto his elbow and forced down on it. Along with the continued twisting of his arm and the general unexpected nature of Betty's actions, the movement caused his feet to leave the sidewalk, and he flew off the edge and lit down hard on the street.

Dusty saw his danger and acted fast. He drew up his left leg and crashed his knee full into the side of Avon's chest. As a grunt of agony burst from the man, Dusty shot up his right arm. He used the *nukite,* piercing hand, thrust, stabbing his extended fingers viciously into Avon's throat. Instantly the hands about his neck loosened, and Avon tumbled over backward. Ignoring Avon for a moment, Dusty rolled onto his left side in time to meet Clayd's attack. Running in, the cowhand drove a kick toward Dusty. Crossing his wrists, Dusty held them so they blocked the kick before it reached him. Then he caught hold of Clayd's leg and pulled him forward. Up snapped Dusty's right leg, the toe of his boot catching Clayd on the inside of the thigh just below the groin. Pain and the twisting heave Dusty gave to the trapped leg sent Clayd tumbling to the ground.

A revolver came from the crowd, landing close to Clayd's side. Snarling in rage, he reached for it. Gun in hand, he sat up and glared at where Dusty rose to deal with Avon. Cocking the gun, Clayd lined it at Dusty's back.

12

"Drop it, Luke!"

At the sound of his boss's voice, Clayd started to look around. Dusty heard the shout and turned. Springing forward, he lashed his boot at Clayd's gun hand, the toe catching it hard and sending the revolver spinning away from its grasp. After yelling his order, Mobstell vaulted the hitching rail and shoved the staggering Avon aside as he tried to reach Dusty. Catching hold of Clayd's shirt collar, Dusty heaved the youngster erect and smashed a punch across to the side of his jaw. Clayd went down as if he had been poleaxed, and a moment later Lynn sprawled on top of him to lie without moving.

Hearing a footstep approaching, Dusty turned ready to continue his defense. He recognized Mobstell and pointed to the revolver lying in the street.

"Your boys said no guns, mister," he said.

"What in hell started this?" demanded the rancher.

"Your boys wanted a fight, and got one."

"Four against two?"

Shaking his head and limping slightly, Red joined his cousin. After sucking in a deep breath, the redhead said, "Shucks, everybody wanted to get into the fun."

"Only I thought we were dealing with square shooters," Dusty stated.

"And?" growled Mobstell.

"That gun there proves some different," Dusty told him. "We left ours behind the bar."

After walking forward, Mobstell picked up the revolver and looked at it. Then he returned, a puzzled expression on his face, and held the gun, butt first, to Dusty.

"Luke uses a Remington," the rancher said. "All the rest of us tote Army Colts."

Studying the gun, Dusty first noticed its five-shot cylinder. True, it looked like a Navy Colt, but that gun carried six, not five, bullets. So Dusty took in the other details: five-and-a-half-inch barrel, brass cone front sight, silver-plated back strap, walnut grips shellacked to a glossy finish, semifluted and rebated cylinder. Even without reading the words METROPOLITAN ARMS CO., NEW YORK, engraved on the barrel, he identified the gun as one of that company's Navy Pocket-model revolvers, imitations of and in competition with the Navy Colt.

"Where'd this come from then?" asked Dusty.

"Somebody in the crowd threw it," Mobstell answered. "From on the porch—"

Both he and Dusty swung toward the porch and found that the marshal, showing a remarkable burst of enthusiasm for his work, had already started to move the crowd off about its business. So effective had he been that people milled and moved on the sidewalk in a manner that prevented Mobstell from indicating who stood in the area from which the gun came.

Suddenly Betty realized that a newly married woman ought to be showing far more concern for her husband's welfare than she had so far. She jumped off the porch, and ran to Red's side.

"Are you hurt, honey?" she gasped. "Landsakes, your face is bleeding."

"I'll do," Red replied.

"Oh, no, you won't," she told him. "You're coming down to the stable now, and we're going home."

"It'd be best," Dusty said. "I'll stay on here for a spell."

"And m—" began Red.

"You will not!" Betty snapped. "You're coming with me."

Red allowed himself to be led off by Betty. Watching them go, Mobstell scratched his head.

"How in Sam Hill did a lil gal like that toss Shanty over her head?" he demanded. "Which same I'll fix his wagon but good when I get him to the ranch, laying hands on her like he done."

"We're a talented family." Dusty smiled. "And I reckon you'll find Cousin Sarah wouldn't want him treated mean on her account. Right now, though, I want to know more about that gun."

"I can't see anybody not wearing one," Mobstell said, scanning the crowd. "Not that that means anything, way they're moving about. You had enough?"

The last was directed at Avon, who walked slowly forward. Rubbing his jaw, the cowhand nodded.

"I'm surely satisfied," he answered, holding his right hand toward Dusty. "Friend, you've sure got an elegant way with you. Say, who did that to you, Shanty?"

"Ain't sure whether there was six or seven of 'em," the bearded hand replied. "Le's help the sleeping beauties rise."

"Don't ask me to kiss either of them awake," said Dusty.

At that moment Stevie came up carrying a bottle of whiskey. "For the victors, with the boss's compliments," she announced.

"Thanks," Dusty answered, drawing the cork. "I need it. These boys can sure fight."

After taking a drink, Dusty passed the bottle to Avon, who wiped the blood from his face and helped himself to a generous drink. Then the cowhand went to assist Shanty with their companions. They lifted Lynn and Clayd to their feet and steered their wobbly legs toward the horse trough outside the blacksmith's shop. While the dazed pair ducked their heads under the water, Avon and Shanty returned to their boss.

"Here, walk down the livery barn and give these to Sandy

McGraw," Mobstell ordered Shanty, holding out Red's hat and gun belt brought from the bar at Stevie's orders.

"M-me?" gulped the bearded cowhand.

"You," confirmed his boss with a dry grin. "And if you come flying through the window, I'll know you ain't learned to keep your hands to yourself yet."

"Sure, boss," Shanty muttered, reluctantly accepting the items. Slowly he turned and ambled off, with more than one backward glance as if in the hope that Mobstell might suffer a change of heart.

"I've seen him bust head down and guns bellowing into a bunch of maybe twenty-thirty Kaddo bucks and not think twice about it," said Mobstell in wonderment. "Say, just *how* in hell did that pretty lil lady toss him over her head?"

"I could tell you better over a drink," Dusty replied, thrusting the Metropolitan revolver into his waistband.

"We all could do with a drink," Stevie said, taking Dusty and Mobstell by the arms. "You owe me one from earlier, too, Cal."

With that she steered the men into the saloon and toward the bar.

At one pound ten ounces weight and ten and five-eighths inches overall length, the Metropolitan was a pound lighter and three and three-eighths inches shorter than the 1860 Army Colt. So it rode light in Dusty's waist band and struck him as being worthy of the name Navy pocket revolver. The Navy part referred to its .36 barrel, that having become accepted as the ideal caliber for use by sailors.

Being intent on studying Mobstell, Dusty gave no thought to the significance of the Metropolitan's characteristics. He wanted to discover what kind of man the rancher might be. The fact had not escaped Dusty that Mobstell might have told his hands to pick a fight if the opportunity arose. Nor did he overlook the possibility that Mobstell had thrown the revolver and shouted too early, meaning to give the order just as Clayd squeezed the trigger. True, Mobstell's Colt still hung in its holster, but a man could easily conceal the Metropolitan; it had been designed with that in mind.

Again something happened to take Dusty's thoughts from the revolver. Collecting his property from the bar, he looked at his reflection in the mirror. Apart from a bruise on his cheek, he had come out of the fight unmarked, but his clothes, face, and hair bore a liberal coating of the plaza's dust.

"I could use a chance to clean up," he remarked.

"Why not come across to my place and do it?" asked Stevie, darting a quick glance around her.

"Do you live here in the saloon?"

"No, Ed. We have a small house out back; all the girls room there. Come on over and tidy up if you like."

Even as she spoke, the girl darted another almost nervous glance around the room and halted it for a moment at the door marked "Private" that Dusty assumed led into Towcester's office. It almost seemed that the girl did not want her boss to see her make the offer.

"Go ahead, Ed," said Mobstell. "Me 'n' the boys'll have that drink with you when you come back."

If he knew cowhands, it would probably be more than one drink, Dusty guessed. So he decided to take the girl's offer, giving Mobstell's bunch time to drink enough for somebody to become loose-tongued. Not even Lynn raised objections as Dusty walked from the room with Stevie on his arm. An admiring grin creased Lynn's face, for nobody had previously managed to get so far with the girl.

"How in hell did I ever think he was small?" Lynn demanded.

"He sure don't fight small," Avon grunted, touching his jaw with a wince of pain. "Boss, he hits near on as hard as you do."

"Let's tip a glass to him then," said Mobstell, pouring out drinks. "Yes, sir, there is one mighty tough *big* man."

Lying some fifty yards behind the saloon, the small house proved to be clean, comfortable—and deserted. Stevie unlocked the front door and led Dusty to her quarters, a suite of three rooms with elegant furnishings. On entering the sitting room section of her suite, the girl closed the door. Then she turned and faced Dusty, looking him over with calculating interest.

"You're strong," she said.

"I figure it's best to be," Dusty answered, putting his hat and gun belt on the table.

The next moment Stevie stood close to him, arms around his neck and mouth reaching hungrily for his. Pure instinct caused Dusty to wrap his arms about the girl's waist as she kissed him passionately. As his grip tightened, Stevie gave a gasp of pain and tried to pull away.

"Did I hurt you?" Dusty asked as the girl took a pace to the rear.

"N-no," she replied, but he guessed that she lied. "I just wondered what kind of cheap lobby lizzy you'd think I was, throwing myself at you like that. Only I just couldn't stop—"

"You've got dust on your face," Dusty told her as the words trailed off.

With a little gasp, Stevie flew to the dressing table in the next room and stared into the mirror. While removing the smudge of dust, she studied Dusty's reflection and watched as he walked toward her with his gun belt in his hand.

"The washroom's through there," she said, indicating a curtained-off alcove. "You can take your shirt off. I won't peek."

It proved to be another lie. Even with the curtains closed, a sufficiently large gap remained for her to watch Dusty remove his shirt and begin to wash. Stripped to the waist, Dusty's muscular development became fully apparent. Stevie took in the width of his shoulders, the bulk of his biceps and powerful forearms, with the strong-fingered hands, realizing how he had come to defeat two larger, heavier men. Then her eyes strayed to the gun belt and its matched Army Colts. Never had she seen such speed as when Dusty had drawn and shot down the hired killer.

Dusty managed to remove the dust at Stevie's washstand and rejoined the girl in the sitting room after drawing on his shirt again. Holding a clothes brush, Stevie walked to meet him.

"Let me help you with the places you can't reach," she said.

"Sure," Dusty said, buckling on his gun belt and allowing the girl to whisk at his back with the brush.

While submitting to Stevie's ministrations, Dusty wondered at her interest in him. From the look of her rooms, she stood high in her employer's favor and would hardly be likely to throw away such luxury for a casual flirtation. Of course, everybody loved a winner, except possibly the losers, and a man who displayed considerable talent could expect the fair sex to take an interest in him. Dusty might have accepted Stevie's actions as normal, but under the prevailing conditions he felt there might be some deeper motive behind her invitation. Anyway, as Mark Counter would have said, finding out should be fun.

Suddenly the room's door burst open, and Towcester lunged through it. Dusty heard Stevie's low gasp of fright as he whirled, and his left-side Colt flicked into his right hand, lining up on the door. Towcester slammed to a halt, his right hand freezing just as it was about to enter the left side of his jacket. For a moment an almost bestial rage twisted the saloonkeeper's face; then it went, to be replaced by his usual expression of polite courtesy.

"I heard a noise in here," he said, speaking slowly as if feeling out his words. "Not knowing you'd left the barroom, Stevie, I thought it might be somebody who'd broken in to steal something."

"Miss Stevie offered to let me clean up a mite," Dusty told him. "Cousin Sarah would sure rawhide me cruel if I'd showed up at the ranch shedding street dust—"

"The barber's playing faro, so Ed couldn't get a bath there," Stevie added. "I thought, him being new in town, that you'd want for me to be neighborly."

Towcester looked at the girl, and Dusty could see her appear to cringe back into herself as if afraid. Having drawn his conclusions from the magnificence of the girl's quarters, Dusty decided that she must be close to Towcester and scared of his jealousy.

"I reckon that I'd best be going back to the bar," he said.

"I'll come with you," Stevie said hurriedly. Although she appeared to have regained control of herself, Dusty sensed her fear. "Those Rocking Rafter boys'll be drinking like the well's gone dry. Or if they're not, I'd best see they start."

While walking toward the door, Dusty saw the Metropolitan

revolver on the table. Picking it up, he turned toward the saloonkeeper.

"Have you ever seen this before?"

"I can't say I have," Towcester answered. "Hell, nearly everybody in the county wears or owns a Colt of one kind or another."

"What kind do you favor, Mr. Towcester?" asked Dusty, giving the man a quick but searching glance and failing to see any sign of a hidden weapon.

"A Remington double derringer," the saloonkeeper replied, slapping his right-side jacket pocket. "I don't often need a gun, and the Remington's all I need."

"Sure," Dusty admitted, not asking to see the gun.

Since its appearance on the market in 1866, the Remington double derringer had rapidly gained favor with gamblers and others who wanted an easily concealed weapon that offered power enough to knock the fight out of an enemy with one shot, yet did not send the bullet through his body and endanger the lives of anybody standing close behind him.

"Let's go have us a drink, Ed," suggested the girl, taking Dusty's arm.

"Let's do that," Dusty replied. "I surely hope that you come along and let me buy you one, friend."

"I've never refused a drink yet." Towcester smiled, although the joviality did not reach his eyes. "Especially when I also get the profit on it being sold."

With that Towcester turned and walked from the room. Followed by Stevie and Dusty, he went to the front door, opened it, and stepped out. A voice called the saloonkeeper's name as he crossed the porch. Looking in the direction of the speaker, Dusty saw the land agent approaching with two sheets of paper clutched in his hand. At the same moment Corlin became aware of Dusty's presence. He slowed down his pace and slipped the papers into his jacket pocket.

"Would Senor Cordova be in the saloon, Mr. Towcester?" Corlin asked.

"No," the saloonkeeper answered. "He rode out of town. Did you want to see him about something?"

"Some business with his ranch," Corlin said. "It'll wait, though."

Watching the land agent turn to depart, Dusty decided to put a thought into practice. Just why, he could not understand, but he went ahead for all that.

"Say, Mr. Corlin," he said. "I've been thinking about that letter Sandy sent to tell you he was coming—"

"Like I said," the land agent interrupted, "it never arrived."

"Sure," said Dusty. "But if it had, there'd've been an easy way to find out if he was Sandy or not."

"How?"

"All you'd needed to do was look at the letter and compare the writing with that on the receipt Sandy signed and you'd be able to see if he was who he claimed to be."

"It's a pity that the letter never reached you then, Mr. Corlin," Towcester remarked. "I know how bad the mail service is, so it doesn't surprise me."

"Still, everybody knows that Sandy really is Sandy now," Dusty went on, watching Corlin's face, "don't they?"

"He proved it pretty conclusively," Towcester said.

"There's no doubt about it," Corlin said. "I'd best go see if any of Cordova's men are at the cantina. My business with him is pretty important."

Watching the land agent scuttle away, Dusty felt sure that the man knew something. Before he could find an excuse to leave the others and follow Corlin, Stevie caught his arm and headed him toward the saloon. Towcester stood for a moment looking after Corlin, then followed the girl and Dusty into the Golden Goose once more.

13

Although Dusty spent an enjoyable afternoon with Mobstell's ranch hands, he learned nothing to help locate the man behind the attempts on Sandy's life. Long practice had taught Dusty to drink sparingly and yet give the appearance of keeping up with his companions' consumption. So he remained sober while his male companions grew more drunk and talkative. Dusty learned much about local conditions and certain items of gossip but could not find a thing either to prove or to disprove Mobstell's connection with the events that had brought the three cousins to San Garcia.

He did learn that Towcester bore a reputation for being bad medicine. After taking one drink with the celebrating group, the saloonkeeper disappeared into his office. Among other items of local gossip, the cowhands warned Dusty not to make any attempt to damage the more lavish fittings of the room. On three occasions, as Stevie had hinted to Red earlier, drunken cowhands had tried to smash the chandelier, and each time

Towcester handed them a beating out of all proportion to the value of his property.

"Mind you, though," Avon told Dusty confidentially, "I reckon you could take him, Ed."

"I don't even feel like trying," Dusty replied and passed the word for the glasses to be filled again.

After collecting his horse from the livery barn later that evening, Dusty rode out of San Garcia. By following the directions Mobstell had given to him, Dusty easily located the Lazy M's headquarters. Night had fallen as Dusty rode toward the cluster of small buildings, but he could see well enough to locate the barn. Unlike the main house, this proved to be made of wood and with sufficient accommodation for half a dozen horses. The house, bunkhouse, and cook shack were all adobe built, small, and set out to offer one another mutual defense, a vital point in the days when marauding Indians and bad Mexicans posed a threat to the lives of people on isolated ranches. Three pole corrals, a small store cabin, and an outhouse completed the ranch's living quarters. All in all, the buildings struck Dusty as being just what a small ranch needed to supply comfort for its owners.

With the big paint stallion settled in a stall, Dusty carried his saddle to the main house. Cactus and Rache had come out on hearing his arrival, telling him that the boss lady wanted to see him. Knowing what to expect, Dusty prepared his defenses even before reaching the house. Beating Betty to the punch, Dusty immediately launched into a description of the happenings in town. While the girl had intended to make known her views on his behavior—having already told Red what she thought of him—she decided to leave it until later.

"Who do you think hired Damon?" she asked as they sat at the table in the living room.

"The same man who hired Murphy," Red answered. "Could be Mobstell, Cordova, the land agent, the saloonkeeper, he's been seen riding around the spread, that lard-gutted marshal—"

"Or somebody we've not met yet and don't know about," Dusty interrupted.

"How do we find out, Dusty?" Betty inquired. "I'd say wait until they make another move, but we can't stay here indefinitely."

"That's for sure," Dusty said. "With Lon, Mark, and Billy Jack all away, I want to get home as soon as I can. Even without Sandy champing on the bit to get here and start running his spread."

"Then what're we going to do?" Red wanted to know.

"I've already started doing it. Unless I'm wrong, that land agent's in this game up to his skinny lil neck. So I prodded him a mite; maybe we'll have some result. I hinted that comparing the signature on that receipt you signed and the letter that never came would have proved who you are, Red."

"So?" Red asked.

"I think he already had compared them," Dusty replied.

"You mean that the letter reached him?" Betty said.

"I'd say so. He looked kind of startled when he saw your signature, was going to say something and didn't. Then later this afternoon he was coming toward the back of the saloon. Called out to Towcester and had two papers in his hand. But he stuffed them away pronto and asked for Cordova."

"You reckon he had Sandy's letter and my receipt?" asked Red.

"I'd bet on it."

"Who was he going to tell?"

"That's the big question, Betty gal," Dusty replied. "Maybe Towcester, only when he saw me he figured to make me think he wanted Cordova."

"What're we going to do, Dusty?" demanded Red, always eager to go into some kind of action.

"Let them stew for a couple of days," Dusty replied. "Then we'll ride into town and see what we can make pop."

The following morning Dusty and Red started a tour of the Lazy M range, acting as a new owner would be expected to do. Nothing Dusty saw helped him to understand why anybody would go to such extremes to gain possession of the property. It was good grazing land, yet no more so than the surrounding country. Returning to the house on the second day, Dusty learned that the ranch had a certain historical significance. As they rode toward the creek which watered the buildings, Cactus indicated it with a touch of pride.

"That was where old Jim Bowie and his boys held off the Kaddos and Kiowas and done sent ole Tres Manos to the Happy Hunting Grounds."

"You can see the bullet holes in the trees and find rusted-up arrerheads," Rache went on. "That's mebbe what that Mexican jasper's looking for."

"Which Mexican?" Dusty asked.

"There's one been watching us both yesterday and today," the old-timer answered calmly. "I've seed him a couple of times, back there a fair piece."

"Why didn't you say something?" Dusty growled.

"Warn't no point. He could see us and'd've run afore we could get close enough to say howdy."

"Want for us to take out after him, Dusty?" Red said hopefully.

"He's pulled out already," Rache commented. "Might be able to follow his sign, though."

"Make a try," Dusty ordered. "I'll go on down to the house."

Half an hour later Red and the old-timers returned to tell how they had lost the mysterious watcher's tracks on some rocky ground, but when last seen, the trail headed toward Cordova's ranch.

"Which proves something," Red finished. "Only what, I don't know."

"Either he works for Cordova and's been sent to watch us," Dusty said, "or he wants us to think he works for Cordova. Say, Red, you remember when that fight Bowie had with the Kaddos happened?"

"On that horse-hunting trip when he was supposed to have found the silver mine," Red replied. "And Murphy was talking about Jim Bowie's lost mine. Aw, hell, Dusty, you don't reckon somebody thinks it's around here?"

"I reckon we'd best ride into town tomorrow," Dusty replied.

Shortly before noon the next day Dusty and Red rode into San Garcia. Passing the Paraiso cantina, they saw a bunch of horses standing at its hitching rail. Judging by the large-horned 'dinner-plate' saddles the horses carried, Cordova's men were in town. Two of the horses, both big, fine-looking animals with costly rigs, caught the eye. However, Dusty and Red did not stop but left their own horses at the livery barn.

Corlin looked up from the papers on his desk as his office door opened.

"Howdy, Mr. Corlin," Red said, entering the room alone.

"Good afternoon, Mr. McGraw," the agent replied. "What can I do for you?"

"I was wanting to know something about the mineral rights to my spread."

"Mi-mineral rights?"

"Sure. You know, like supposing gold's discovered on my range, is it mine no matter who finds it?"

For a moment Corlin did not reply, but his face worked nervously. Then he made an effort and regained control of himself.

"I hardly think it's likely—" he began.

"Maybe not," Red drawled. "But I'd sure like to know."

"Mineral rights are a tricky subject," Corlin told him. "I'd have to read up the various rulings before I can give you a clear explanation. The books are in my room at the saloon. It may take some considerable time."

"I'll be around for a spell," Red told him. "Say, does the general store sell blasting powder, picks, and shovels?"

"I believe they may have a keg in—"

"I'll need a whole lot more than one keg. Got a whole slew of tree stumps around the place that want clearing off."

Red said the second sentence in the manner of an afterthought as if he had suddenly realized that the first gave too much information. Nodding to the land agent, he walked from the office, his whole attitude that of a man wishing to avoid answering inconvenient questions. Although he did not look back, Red guessed that Corlin watched him from the office window and so headed straight for the general store.

A short time later Corlin left the small building that housed his office. He darted a nervous glance in each direction before hurrying off along the street. Stepping out of the alley where he had been standing to avoid being seen, Dusty followed Corlin to the Golden Goose saloon. Looking through one of the front windows, Dusty was in time to see the agent going upstairs.

Stevie rose from the table where she sat with a couple of the girls as Dusty entered the barroom. Crossing the floor, she smiled a greeting.

"Hey, there, Ed," she said, "I was beginning to think you'd forgotten me."

"I've been busy out at the spread," Dusty replied. "Come and have a drink."

"That's what I'm here for," she answered.

"Say, Stevie," Dusty said as they stood at the bar with their drinks, "I've been thinking about moving into town. Where can I find a room?"

"Here. It's as near to a hotel as this one-hoss town's got."

"Many folks use it?"

"The marshal, the land agent, folks passing through."

"I reckon I'll see Towcester about it," Dusty said. "Where is he?"

"In his office," the girl replied, then went on as Dusty put his glass down. "Tony's busy just now. You'll have to see him later."

"Sure," Dusty said. "Say, was I to come and live here, could I get out of my room without using the stairs there? I mean, if I wanted to meet *somebody* private like."

"Only by climbing down the fire rope in your room," the girl replied. "And who would you be wanting to see private like?"

"A real pretty lil gal I know," Dusty told her with a wink. "Have another drink."

"I've never refused. Hey, here's your boss."

After entering the saloon, Red walked across to the bar. "I've got it all ordered like you said, Ed. Man, oh, man, just think. All those years and ole Uncle Seth never knew about it. You figured it out mighty slick from what that dying gunny told—"

"You've got a big mouth, Sandy!" Dusty growled.

"What's wrong, Ed?" Stevie asked.

"Nothing," Dusty answered, throwing a scowl at Red.

"Will you be able to afford to come and live in town?" she inquired.

"He sure will after we—" Red began.

"Get the spread going!" Dusty interrupted. "Don't you want to see the land agent, Sandy?"

"Sure. Which room's he in, Stevie?"

"The third on the left at the front."

Dusty and Stevie carried on a conversation while Red disappeared upstairs, but the girl made no further reference to the hints given by the cousins. After a short time Red returned.

"He's not there. Or if he is, he's deaf. I knocked hard."

"Maybe Stevie can help us," Dusty remarked. "Do you know anybody around here that's done any mining?"

"Mi-mining?" she gasped. "I can't think of anybody. What do you want with a miner?"

"If this ranch business doesn't pay off, I aim to go up north to the gold camps and try my luck," Dusty told her. "Figured I might as well learn something about the game afore I sat in on it."

"Oh!" she said in the kind of tone women always use when being told a lie.

All the time they talked Dusty had a feeling of being watched. Years of riding danger trails had developed in him an instinct for such things. Unless he missed his guess, somebody was studying the three of them with hostile eyes. Yet he could not locate the watcher. Before he could set about discovering who took such an interest in them, Dusty saw Corlin come down the stairs. Without a glance at the cousins, Corlin walked from the saloon.

"Well, I'll be damned," Red said. "He was up there all the time."

"He may have been with Vinnie, one of the girls," Stevie answered. "They see a lot of each other."

"Reckon I'll go have a talk with him," Red drawled. "Coming, Cousin—Ed?"

"I reckon I'll stay here and talk to Stevie instead," Dusty replied.

Although Red left the saloon soon after Corlin, he made no attempt to catch up to the man. Instead he tagged along at a short distance behind Corlin until the land agent entered the Paraiso cantina. Walking along, Red glanced through the window and saw Corlin join Cordova. On the land agent's arrival, the two vaqueros seated at the rancher's table rose and walked over to their companions at the bar. Standing by the side of the window, Red watched Corlin sit down and start to talk with Cordova.

"Why don't you go in, gringo, instead of standing outside and spying?" said a voice.

Turning, Red looked at a stocky, swarthy Mexican whose evil face did not go with the once elegant but now dirty clothing of a caballero. No gun hung at the man's side, only a long bladed fighting knife.

"Says which?" asked Red.

"I don't like gringos spying on my boss," the Mexican growled, and put his left hand on Red's shoulder. "Get—"

Red knocked the hand aside and saw the right start to move toward the knife's hilt. Guessing that the knife would prove just as deadly as a gun in the man's hand, Red hit him before his fingers closed on its handle. Back shot the Mexican and landed rump first on the sidewalk. Spanish curses roared from the man's lips, and he started to rise, reaching for the knife again.

"Leave it be," Red said, backing his order up with his left-hand Colt's cocking click as he drew and aimed down on the Mexican.

Behind Red, the cantina doors opened, and some of Cordova's men appeared. Attracted by the man's shouted curses, more of the cantina's customers followed the vaqueros, and Red could hear their excited comments.

"You're a brave man with a gun in your hand, gringo!" the Mexican spat out. "Like all your kind. Without the gun you are nothing. I, Manuel Ortega, spit on you."

"Maybe you'd like me to put the gun away," Red replied, twirling it back into the leather.

"What does that mean?" Ortega snarled. "If I try to avenge the insult you put on me, you will shoot me down."

"You got a notion on how you'd like to get satisfaction for the insult?" asked Red, plunging into what he guessed to be a trap.

"With a knife!"

Despite his hotheaded way of becoming involved in fights, Red never went completely blind-charging. He guessed that Ortega intended to force a fight, but he refused to back down. Yet Red knew the danger all too well. Having seen that master of the knife-fighting art, the Ysabel Kid, in action, Red did not underestimate the peril. Swiftly he sought for a way to counter Ortega's challenge. An idea sprang to Red's mind, although it was not one a more prudent man would have considered. Of course, a prudent man would not find himself in such a situation.

"All right, *hombre,*" he said. "We'll use knives, if somebody'll lend me one. Only we'll do it a way that'll give me an even chance."

"How's that?" Ortega asked, showing surprise at Red's acceptance.

"Helena-fashion," Red replied.

Shock wiped the sneer from Ortega's face, and Red's words were repeated in hushed tones among the crowd. Any of the onlookers who did not know what Red meant rapidly had the deficiency rectified by the more knowledgeable present. A Helena duel meant that the two contestants stood in a twenty-foot circle, each holding a knife in one hand, their other wrists fastened together. On the signal to start being given, they went at it and remained fastened together until one of them could not continue.

"You mean to go through with this, senor?" asked Cordova.

"All the way," Red said. "This *pelado*'s* been hired to pick a fight with me, and I aim to get it done here, not have him waiting to backshoot me some dark night."

"You lie, gringo!" Ortega snarled. "But soon it will not matter. The insult will be wiped out in your blood."

No man of Cordova's upbringing would attempt to stop an affair of honor. So, although a hint of concern flickered across his handsome face, he gave the order for a circle to be made ready. Then he turned to his *segundo* and told the man to lend Red a knife.

Looking confident, Ortega swaggered into the circle a vaquero traced in the dirt of the street. He held his knife in his right hand, extending the left toward Red.

"Looks like we've got us a problem," Red said quietly. "I'm left-handed."

Having used his right fist to knock the Mexican down, Red had drawn his left-side Colt as being more readily available. However, the fact that he had used his left hand added strength to his statement. Studying the clumsy manner in which Red held the borrowed knife, Ortega shrugged and agreed to change hands. Showing no emotion, Jesus, Cordova's *segundo,* fastened the two right wrists together in such a way that each man could grasp the other's forearm in his hand.

Already word of the trouble had reached the Golden Goose saloon, causing Dusty to leave it hurriedly. Followed by a number of interested people, Dusty headed for the cantina. He saw Corlin approaching and noticed that Dr. Paczek stood outside a store watching him. Ignoring the land agent, Dusty continued to walk toward the growing circle of men and women before the cantina. Then he heard a voice snap out the word *Fight!* and knew he could not arrive in time to help his cousin, even assuming that Red would want him to do so.

As Ortega watched Red and waited for Cordova to give the command to fight, his fingers tightened slightly on the Texan's arm. When the word came to start, the Mexican heaved in an

* Pelado: Used in such a manner, it means graverobber.

attempt to drag his opponent off-balance. Ortega prepared for resistance to the pull, but Red's move took Ortega completely by surprise, for Red came forward—and fast. Perhaps using his knife right-handed, as he usually did, Ortega could have countered the move. Holding his weapon in the left hand confused him for that vital split second Red needed to attack.

Red let Jesus's knife fall from his hand as he went forward. Once again his fist lashed into Ortega's face, striking the nose with some force. Pain blinded Ortega, throwing his thought patterns all ways. Nor did he find time to recover. Down whipped Red's left hand, driving hard knuckles full into Ortega's belly with sickening force. Breath rushed from Ortega's mouth, and his body hunched over, presenting his jaw to Red's fist as it came up to meet him. Lifted erect again, Ortega stood dazed, blinded by tears brought by the pain of his broken, blood-squirting nose, wide open for the backhand smash Red sent to the underside of his jaw. The knife fell from Ortega's fingers, and he started to fall backward. Only the support given to him by being fastened to Red prevented him from crashing to the ground.

Bending down, Red let Ortega subside and took up the borrowed knife. Silence dropped on the crowd as they waited to see what Red meant to do next. Under the free-and-easy rules of the Helena duel, he could finish off his enemy any way he chose. Slipping the clipped point of the knife between the wrists, he cut the thong holding them together.

"Tell him the next time he crosses me to be wearing a gun," Red said as he handed the knife back to its owner.

"You played that smart, amigo," Cordova remarked, an admiring grin on his face. "Any other way and he would have killed you. Then there would have been bad trouble between your people and mine. May I offer you a drink?"

"I reckon I could use one," Red admitted, seeing Dusty coming through the crowd. "Did anybody ever tell me that I'm loco?"

"If they didn't," Dusty replied before Cordova could speak, "Cousin Be—Sarah's sure going to when she hears about this."

"Now I *do* need that drink," Red stated, glancing at the groaning, writhing Ortega. "How about him?"

"He can buy his own when he recovers," Cordova answered. "In some other town for preference. Jesus, see that he gets on his horse and goes."

"*Sí, señor,*" said the *segundo,* sheathing his knife and leaning against the cantina wall.

Along the street Corlin stood with Paczek, looking toward where the crowd dispersed. An angry snort broke from the doctor.

"That was a fine way for him to act. I thought he would at least try to stop the fight."

"To save his cousin?" Corlin asked, realizing the doctor meant Dusty, not Red.

"To do his duty as a peace officer!" snorted Paczek. "If a Texas Rangers' captain condones brawling in the street, is there any wonder that local peace officers allow it to go on?"

Although Corlin had intended to walk on, he halted and stared at Paczek. "Do you mean that Marsden is a Ranger captain?"

"He told me so himself," Paczek replied, getting his facts wrong in his indignation. Then he remembered Dusty's request. "You will treat this as confidential, won't you?"

"I will," said Corlin, and whirled around as a shot thundered along the street.

14

"Will you gentlemen both take a drink with me?" Cordova asked. "I feel that we should get acquainted as we are to be neighbors."

"We'll be pleased to, senor," Dusty replied.

"Here, or at the Golden Goose?"

"Here's fine," Dusty told the rancher.

Turning, Cordova led the way into the cantina. As Dusty and Red neared its doors, they heard startled gasps and exclamations behind them, mingled with the sound of hurriedly moving feet. Recognizing what the sounds meant, each cousin began to swing around and sent a hand streaking toward its gun. Before either completed his turn, a shot thundered out.

Jesus stood with a smoking Colt in his hand, its barrel slanting down toward the street. Sprawled on his back, a hole between his eyes and a Remington double derringer lying alongside his right hand, Ortega kicked his life away.

"You didn't hit him hard enough, senor," the *segundo* remarked calmly.

"That is true," Cordova went on. "His kind do not forgive easily. Sooner or later you would have had to kill him."

"Likely," Red answered. *"Gracias,* Jesus."

"If a man starts a fight with a knife, he should end it with one, senor," the *segundo* replied.

"Does he mean me or that Ortega jasper?" Red inquired as he followed Cordova into the cantina.

"A little of both probably." The rancher smiled. "Jesus belongs to the old school and feels you have gone against the code duello in fighting the way you did. Not that I blame you."

Dusty stayed at the cantina's door so as to hear what happened when the town marshal came to investigate the shooting. On his arrival Tenby looked at the body and shrugged.

"Just a greaser killing," he said. "Who done it?"

"I did," Jesus replied coldly.

"Figure you'd a good enough reason," Tenby growled. "Get him off the street pronto."

"And that is all it matters!" Jesus spit out as the marshal ambled away.

"Not all lawmen are like him, amigo," Dusty pointed out. "Do you know the dead man?"

"I've never seen him before," Jesus replied. "Even if he is another of us greasers."

"The marshal said it, not me," Dusty said quietly. "There're good and bad in every race."

"Sí, señor. And this is one of the bad ones. I will see to him. My patron wishes to speak with you."

"See if you can learn who he is and where he's been for me, will you?"

"I will try to learn, senor," Jesus promised.

Entering the cantina, Dusty joined Red and Cordova at the bar. Although Jesus returned after taking the body to the undertaker's shop and announced that nobody appeared to know where Ortega came from, the rest of the afternoon passed pleasantly enough. Cordova proved to be an excellent host. However, as in Mobstell's case, Dusty could find nothing to point to

Cordova's being the man behind Sandy's troubles. At sundown Dusty and Red left the cantina and walked through the town in the direction of the livery barn. On the way Red told Dusty the full story of the events leading to his fight with Ortega, having left out certain points while talking about it to Cordova.

"What do you make of it, Dusty?" he asked as they saddled their horses. "Ortega allowed I was spying on his boss."

"He could've been telling the truth, figuring you'd be too dead to mention it later," Dusty replied. "Or he said it so you'd think Cordova hired him."

"His hoss was outside the cantina. I saw them load him onto it and tote him away."

"And there was that Mexican jasper watching us at the ranch."

"Cordova'd likely hire Mexicans rather than white folks," Red pointed out.

"So would somebody who wanted us to blame Cordova for sending a hired gun after you," Dusty said.

"This whole damned game's sickening my guts," Red growled. "Give me a face-to-face, straight-up fight any time."

"Sure," Dusty said. "Only we have to play it the way whoever we want deals the hand."

As the cousins led their horses from the barn, they saw the Golden Goose's swamper approaching.

"Miss Stevie wants to see you, Mr. Marsden," the old-timer said.

"I'm just headed back to the spread," Dusty replied.

"She said to tell you it's real important."

"You'd maybe best go, Du—Ed," Red said. "I'll head back to the spread."

"Sure," Dusty replied. "Only ride careful and don't go to sleep in the saddle. Unless it's something real important, I'll try to catch up with you on the way home."

Red mounted his claybank, and Dusty watched him ride off. Wondering what the girl might want, Dusty left his horse saddled but in the livery barn. On reaching the saloon, he saw Stevie at the bar. She walked toward him as he entered, smiling with her lips only. While her face bore its usual makeup, there was a puffiness about the eyes as if she had been crying recently.

"Hi!" Dusty greeted her. "What'd you want to see me about?"

"I—I thought you'd want to see me before you left town," she replied, darting a glance in Towcester's direction. Then she dropped her voice and turned her back on the saloonkeeper. "I've found that miner for you."

"Where is he?" Dusty asked.

"At the house. I thought you'd not want folks to see you talking to him or they might get the wrong idea."

"Smart thinking," Dusty said. "Let's go see him."

"C-can't we have a drink first?"

Something in the girl's attitude disturbed Dusty. It almost seemed that she did not want to go with him. After crossing to the bar, he ordered a couple of drinks and looked at Towcester. Nodding a greeting, the saloonkeeper went to watch a game of cards being played at one of the tables.

"Well," Dusty said to the girl as they finished their drinks, "how about this miner?"

Looking past him for a moment, the girl gulped and nodded. "All right, we'll go and see him."

"Let's do—" Dusty began.

"Not together!" Stevie interrupted. "Tony's jealous already. After you leave, I'll slip out of the back door and meet you by the house."

"We'll do that," Dusty said, and raised his voice. "Much as I'd like to, I can't stay any longer, Stevie. I'll see you the next time I'm in town."

"I'll be here," the girl replied, and seemed about to say more, but Towcester left the card game and walked in her direction.

Strolling from the saloon, Dusty turned along the sidewalk. He paused at the window and looked inside. Already Stevie had made her way toward the rear door and Towcester had gone into his office. Slowly Dusty continued along the front of the saloon, passed through the alley separating it from the next building, and halted at the rear while he studied the area ahead of him. Both the back of the saloon and the small house were in darkness. Dusty could see nothing to disturb his peace of mind and so stepped forward.

A shape rose on the porch of the house. Instantly Dusty stopped. Then he saw the white V a shirt made when worn under a buttoned-up jacket. Clearly the man on the porch expected somebody, for he stepped forward. Even as Dusty recognized the man as Corlin, a shot crashed from the other end of the saloon. Jerking backward, Corlin slammed into the wall and slid down.

Although Dusty's right hand fetched out the left-side Colt without conscious thought on his part, he did not squeeze the trigger. For one thing he could see nothing to shoot at; also, he wanted to reach Corlin and learn how badly the man was hit. After darting to the house, Dusty bounded up onto the porch and knelt at Corlin's side. A glance at the place from where the shot had come failed to reveal any sign of the man responsible. Then Dusty turned his attention to Corlin. Whoever had fired the shot knew his business. Before Dusty could do more than look, Corlin gave a harsh, rattling cough. The land agent's body twisted convulsively and then went limp.

At the same moment Dusty heard a soft footstep at the end of the building. Looking up, he saw the bulky shape of the marshal and recognized the thing in Tenby's hands. Maybe Tenby lacked most of the qualities one expected in a lawman, but he knew the correct tool for his present work. He was also, Dusty concluded, deeply involved in Corlin's murder. Instead of looking to where the shot had been fired, Tenby stared first to where Dusty might be expected to have halted and then swiveled himself around to face the porch.

Flinging himself aside and down, Dusty saw flame belch from the muzzle of Tenby's shotgun. Something struck the planks just behind the small Texan as he rolled off the porch and at the same time he heard the sinister, eerie whistle as more .32-caliber buckshot balls fanned the air above him. If he had reacted just a shade more slowly, he would have been caught in the shotgun's deadly nine-ball pattern. Still, Dusty did not shoot. On landing upon the ground, he twisted himself back under the porch and edged in beneath it. Over his head heavy boots thudded on the porch's planks. On the plaza voices yelled. The saloon's side doors burst open, and men started to come out and ran toward the rear of the building. Coming to a halt, Tenby peered cautiously over the porch rail and cursed when he did not see Dusty's body. Having jumped down, as people converged on the house, Tenby glanced under the edge of the porch. He failed to see Dusty and straightened up to answer a request to be told who had done the shooting.

"That Ed Marsden's just killed Agent Corlin," Tenby replied. "Shot him down in cold blood and him without a gun."

"Why'd Marsden do a thing like that?" demanded a voice Dusty recognized as belonging to the Wells Fargo agent.

"Maybe I can tell you," Towcester answered. "Mr. Corlin told me earlier tonight that he had learned the man claiming to be Sandy McGraw is an impostor."

"Who is he?" asked one of the crowd.

"We don't know yet," Towcester replied. "But we shall when the marshal gets his hands on Marsden. Where is he now, Marshal?"

"He took off running, went 'round the corner there," Tenby answered.

"You mean that you missed him—with a shotgun?" the saloonkeeper growled.

"Hell, it was dark on the porch, Mr. Towcester," Tenby said. "You've seen how fast he can move. I didn't have time to—"

"You'll have to find and arrest him," Towcester pointed out.

"Yeah."

Indecision showed in the one-word answer given by the marshal. Clearly he did not relish the thought of tangling with "Ed Marsden." An angry snort broke from Towcester's lips as he read worry and not a little fear in Tenby's attitude.

"All right, boys," Towcester told the assembled crowd. "The marshal wants deputies, and none of us can blame him when he's got to deal with a gunslick like Marsden. I've not liked the way Marsden's been acting since he came here. So I'll give any man who comes forward a free night's drinking in my place."

Dusty had noticed that the Golden Goose's clientele that night included a good number of the usual type of range loafers, the kind of men who would do anything except work for a night's free drinking. So Tenby did not lack volunteers, although several members of the crowd held back.

"All right," Tenby growled when sure he would raise no more help. "Two of you go to the livery barn and watch his hoss. The rest of you split up and start looking for him."

"You've forgotten something, Marshal," Towcester interrupted. "Marsden's a killer, and you don't want any of these good gents gunned down. So make sure they know not to take chances."

"Yeah," Tenby said. "If you boys see Marsden, shoot first and ask questions after he's dead."

Lying beneath the porch, Dusty watched the crowd separate and depart. Everything began to flop into place; all the puzzling aspects of the affair grew more clear in the light of the new developments. There were a few gaps to fill in, but Dusty felt sure that Towcester was the man behind the hired gun who had tried to kill Sandy McGraw.

Although Dusty hoped for a chance to reach Towcester, the saloonkeeper returned to the Golden Goose before the crowd dispersed. While waiting for a chance to leave his place, Dusty decided against bursting in on Towcester straight away. The element of surprise might be on Dusty's side, but there were too many people in town ready to shoot him down for him to take risks. First he must escape, go to the ranch, and gather reinforcements. Then he could have a showdown with Towcester.

Easing himself from under the porch, Dusty made a cautious way along the back street in the direction of the livery barn. Once he crouched in the darkness while a trio of Tenby's "deputies" passed by in what they imagined to be a conscientious search.

As usual the livery barn was illuminated by a couple of oil lamps, and Dusty, looking in through the rear window, saw two men sitting on a bale of hay. Neither appeared to be taking his duty too seriously, nor had they interfered with the big paint. Not that Dusty felt surprised at the latter, knowing his horse's temperament and general distrust of strangers. Carefully Dusty inched open the barn's rear door and stepped in with his left hand filled with its Colt.

"Just sit still, boys," he ordered as the men started to turn. "If you aim to move or shout, pray first."

Two startled faces swiveled in Dusty's direction. Although the men sat as if turned to stone, one of them began to open his mouth.

"I wouldn't," Dusty advised, making a convincing gesture with his Colt, and the mouth closed again. "Now both of you take out your guns and see how far you can throw them into the stalls—left-handed, hombre. That way you'll live to earn your night's free drinking." The last came as one of the pair reached gunward with his right hand. Awkwardly drawing his gun, the man flipped it across the barn to fall into a stall. A moment later his companion's weapon disappeared into the straw at the other side. "Now lie flat on your bellies," Dusty said.

After one look at his grimly set face, the two men obeyed. After walking to his paint, Dusty tested the saddle, and satisfied that he could mount without the saddle slipping because of its girths being loosened, he took the reins in his right hand. Watching the men, he led the horse across the barn and halted at the rear door.

"Don't come rushing to see me off, boys," he warned, and vaulted into the saddle.

Giving the men no chance to make a hostile move, Dusty started the paint moving. He did not know what kind of conditions he might meet on the back streets and decided against risking laming his horse. So he swung the paint between two buildings and reached the main street. He set his spurs to the big horse's flanks and started it galloping. Behind him a voice yelled, then more. Two shots crashed, but Dusty did not hear their bullets. Then he passed the last houses, and the darkness swallowed him up as the paint galloped along the Lazy M trail.

A mile from San Garcia, Dusty eased the paint to a halt and sat listening for sounds of pursuit from town. Although he could hear none behind him, hooves drummed on the trail ahead. Nobody from town could have passed him, riding across

country, without his being aware of it. Nor did he believe
Tenby possessed sufficient experience or reasoning ability to
send men out with the intention of cutting off the way to the
Lazy M. For all that, Dusty took no chances. Ahead of him a
clump of bushes offered a hiding place, and he rode toward
them. Slipping from his saddle, Dusty held the paint's head
ready to silence any sound it made.

Three riders came along the trail, moving at a purposeful trot
and in silence. Despite the darkness, Dusty recognized them.
He started to whistle the opening bars of "Dixie." Instantly the
trio halted, Red Blaze and old Cactus swinging their horses in
front of Betty Hardin, and each reached for his favorite
weapon.

"You're jumpy tonight," Dusty said.

"Dusty?" Red asked.

"You're expecting maybe Robert E. Lee?" Dusty replied, and
rode from behind the bushes. "Where do you three reckon
you're going?"

"Into San Garcia to save you from being lured into a life of
sin," Betty told him as Red holstered his revolver and Cactus
replaced the Colt rifle across his knees. "I'm sure Aunt Betty
wouldn't approve of that Stevie Cameron as a daughter-in-
law."

"I'll tell you something," Dusty drawled. "*I* don't approve
too strong of her myself. She tried to make herself a widow
even afore we got to church."

15

"I think you'd better tell us about it," Betty remarked.

"Let's get off the trail first," Dusty suggested.

"Ain't as smart as I used to be—" Cactus began.

"And you never were," Betty interrupted.

"Which same when I was young, a gal knowed her place and didn't speak 'cepting when spoke to. But like I was saying afore I was interrupted, I ain't as smart as I used to be, but I'd allow you've had a mite of trouble, Cap'n Dusty."

Once clear of the trail, Dusty verified Cactus's statement. Quickly he told of the incident in town, from meeting Stevie to his escape. At the end he asked what had brought his cousins and Cactus to the scene.

"We were looking for you," Betty explained, "bringing some interesting news. While Cactus ain't as smart as he used to be, he once in a while uses his head for something besides a peg to hang that smelly old hat on—"

"It ain't so smelly at that," Cactus objected. "Anyways,

Cap'n, me 'n' Rache goes out this morning and combs the area where we lost that greaser's tracks yesterday. Found 'em in the end, only they weren't headed for Cordova's spread—"

"They were coming to town," Dusty guessed.

"Ain't no use trying to surprise these uppy young uns." Cactus sniffed.

"Tell him the rest of it and see," Betty said.

"We follows the trail for a spell, it heading for town all the time, and finds a place where that 'greaser' gets off his hoss to tighten a girth. Must've been after dark, or he'd got careless. Left a good clear footprint—"

"Have your moment of glory." Dusty sighed. "But the night's going fast."

"That 'greaser,' Cap'n," Cactus replied. "Turns out he warn't wearing range boots, but low-heeled town redjacks.*

"Which same Ortega had range boots on," Red added.

Range boots invariably bore high heels to give the wearer a better grip of the stirrup irons or to allow him to dig into the ground when holding back on a roped animal while afoot. Being designed for walking rather than horseback work, town footwear had low heels.

"We'd best go back into town," Dusty stated.

"Straight down the main drag, heads held high and chests puffed out in righteous pride?" Red asked.

"Waal, no," Dusty replied. "I was thinking more of sneaking in on foot. And don't you worry none, we'll ride as close as we can."

Frenchy Becque stiffened in his chair at the telegraph table as he heard a gentle knock at the door. Having scooped up his revolver, he crossed the room.

"Who is it?"

"Dusty Fog."

Shoving the revolver into his waistband, Becque drew open the door and stood aside to let Betty and the three men enter. A blocky black-haired man with a heavy mustache, Becque man-

---

* Redjacks: Light, waterproof leather boots.

aged to look French even clad in range clothes. His eyes went from one to another of the visitors, admiration flickering at Betty's buckskin jacket, male shirt, and Levi's pants, and taking in the saddle guns each man carried. Quickly he closed the door and watched Dusty lean the Winchester carbine against the wall.

"They've stopped looking for you, Cap'n Fog," Becque said. "And none of 'em rode out after you."

"You know why they're after me?" asked Dusty.

"They say you killed Agent Corlin," Becque replied, and tensed slightly as the matched Colts left Dusty's holsters.

Twirling the guns, Dusty held them butts first to Becque. "Look them over."

While Becque examined the Colts, Dusty removed his gun belt. When the Wells Fargo official offered to return the guns, the small man shook his head.

"Have they been used tonight?" Dusty asked.

"Nor all day at least," Becque replied.

Black powder made a considerable mess when exploding, and nobody, not even the fabled Rio Hondo gun wizard, could have cleaned the two Colts so effectively in the dark or in the time since his hurried departure from town. Pretty convincing proof to Becque's mind, especially when he had not believed Dusty guilty in the first place.

"Then put them in your safe and lock it," Dusty said.

"What?" Becque almost yelped, and the other three also showed surprise.

"Lock them in the safe," Dusty repeated. "Folks in this town think I killed a man in cold blood, and I want to prove I didn't. Showing them that my guns haven't been fired ought to do it."

"Sure, but—" Becque began.

"Just look at my carbine, too, but I'll be needing it," Dusty interrupted.

"So *that's* why you brought it along," Betty whispered.

"I telegraphed Sheriff Washbourne," Becque remarked as he checked that the carbine had not been fired. "Was waiting for an answer when you came in. Who do you reckon's behind this business, Cap'n?"

"Towcester and the marshal," Dusty replied. "Proving it's going to be the hard part."

At that moment the telegraph key started to click, and Becque crossed to its table. He laid aside Dusty's carbine and started to write down the message flashed over the wires.

"It's from Wash," he said. "Tells me to take whatever action I figure's needed. So tell me what you want me to do."

"I'd like to know what Towcester's doing first," Dusty remarked. "Only it won't be safe for any of us to walk the streets."

"Then stay here and I'll go," Becque answered. "I do it every night, so nobody'll think anything should they see me."

As a result of Becque's report on his return, Dusty's party made plans and set off to carry them out. It seemed that Towcester had entertained a number of Tenby's unofficial deputies at the Golden Goose, honoring the promise of free drinks. At least fifteen men remained in the saloon, although all the paying customers had left. Becque's views on the type of men in the saloon was uncomplimentary to them, although true. Guessing that Towcester kept the men around as protection against his return with reinforcements from the Lazy M, Dusty based his strategy on something more Becque told him. Although Dusty wanted Becque to remain in the Wells Fargo building, the man refused.

"I've been pulling down a deputy's pay for a fair time, Cap'n," he said. "It's time I earned some of it."

Stevie Cameron stirred uneasily in her bed as the room's lamp flared up. "Wh-what now, Tony?" she began, then jerked into a sitting position and stared at her visitor. "You!"

"Me," said Betty Hardin. "Get up, Stevie, dear, we're going to have a little talk."

On learning that Stevie had already left the saloon, although the other girls remained to entertain the customers and share their boss's unusual bounty, Betty insisted on being given a chance to interview her. Knowing his cousin's strength of will when she made her mind up, Dusty arranged his plans to satisfy her. Nobody saw the party moving through the streets, and they found the house door open. That did not surprise them, but none expected to have the good fortune of Stevie's suite being unlocked. They came prepared to break open the girl's room and were grateful that the need did not arise. Inside the suite Betty insisted that the men leave Stevie's interrogation to her.

"Get out of here!" Stevie growled, throwing back the covers and starting to rise. She wore a nightdress of more flimsy material than Betty had ever seen.

As Stevie came to her feet, Betty glided in a step. Up lashed Betty's hand in a *nukite* thrust, driving the stiff fingers under Stevie's unprotected left breast. A gasp of agony tore from Stevie. Clutching at her bust, she spun around and collapsed on to the bed with her body twisting in suffering.

"Come on now!" Betty snapped, gripping Stevie's shoulder and dragging her around. The material of the nightdress ripped, baring Stevie's left breast, as she turned. "I didn't hit you that hard! Oh, my Lord!"

The last words came as Betty saw the vicious bruising on the lower side of the breast and mottling the white flesh as far as she could see.

"He never marked me where it showed," Stevie gasped, sitting on the bed.

"Did Towcester do it to you?" Betty asked, her voice brittle.

"He'd've killed any other man who laid hands on me," Stevie replied bitterly. "Tony's full of husbandly love."

"I hope you're not, because I aim to have the truth out of you. Even if I have to knock it out. And you don't look in any shape for rolling around on the floor wrestling."

True enough in view of the bruising Stevie's body showed. In addition, she remembered how the small girl before her had tossed the 190-pound cowhand through the air as if he had weighed no more than a feather.

"If I yell—" Stevie began.

"Try it!" Betty challenged. "You helped set up my cousin Dusty like a stool bird and I don't like that one little bit."

"Dusty? Do you mean Ed Marsden?"

"His name is Dusty Fog."

"Dusty Fog!" Stevie gasped. "Then he's not a Texas Ranger captain."

"Did you think he was?"

"Corlin told Tony that he'd heard Ed was a captain in the Texas Rangers. He was running scared, Corlin, I mean. That was why he was killed."

"And you helped blame Dusty for it!" Betty hissed.

"Have you ever had a man take hold of your apples and crush them as hard as he could?" Stevie spit back, involuntarily touching her bruised breast. "Or sit on your belly and hold a pillow over your face until you're unconscious?"

"No," said Betty in a small voice.

"Then don't blame me for doing what I did. I took a beating this afternoon before I'd agreed to go along with Tony's game. Even though I thought Ed—Dusty—was a Ranger captain."

"Did that make any difference?" Betty asked.

"I killed a drunk in Houston. He was trying to force me into bed with him, and I pushed him away. He hit his head as he fell. Only the Gabrielle family aren't going to let any calico cat get away with killing their son."

"When was this?"

"A year ago."

"You're sure it was Con Gabrielle?"

"I knew him—" Stevie began.

"And so do I," Betty interrupted. "In fact, I threw him off the porch back home not three months ago. He had the same general idea with us both."

For a moment the meaning of the words did not seem to strike Stevie. Then she gasped, "But Tony told me— He was in the next room and came in just after Con hit the floor. No wonder I never saw anything in the papers, although I've never been one for reading. All this time he's been using me. Him and his 'Let's get married, Stevie. A husband can't testify against his wife.' The lousy—"

"And he said he would tell Dusty, or Captain Marsden of the Rangers, about you unless you helped him?"

"Sure. I wanted to warn Ed, but the bartender was too close and kept his sawed-off shotgun in his hand under the counter.

If Ed didn't go along, the bar dog was to shoot him. At least outside Ed had a chance."

"Some chance!" Betty spit out.

"It was better than none," Stevie replied. "And I knew what would happen to *me* if anything went wrong."

"I don't blame you too much." Betty smiled. "Get dressed, and I'll have Dusty in to ask you some questions. If you want to answer, that is."

"Do I want to!" Stevie muttered. "You just give me half a chance."

Drawing on a robe, Stevie sat down. She looked uneasy and not a little frightened when Dusty entered the room. Cold gray eyes raked her from head to foot, and she writhed under the scorn in them.

"And before you start on her, don't!" Betty snapped at her cousin. "I'd've probably done exactly the same as she did had I been treated as she has."

"I'll mind it," Dusty replied. "All right, Stevie. Tell us about Jim Bowie's lost mine."

"You know about it then?" the girl asked.

"I figure it's at the back of all this fuss," Dusty admitted.

"Tony thinks he can locate it somewhere on the Lazy M. But he's not sure where, and it will take a heap of work to find it. That's why he wanted to buy the ranch, so he can do his searching in secret."

"Only Seth McGraw wouldn't sell," Dusty stated. "Did Towcester kill him?"

"I think so," Stevie replied. "Seth looked all right when he came into the bar that day—"

"He'd been complaining about a pain in his guts all morning, Cap'n," Cactus called from where he stood at the sitting room window and watched the rear of the saloon.

"It could be that Towcester got lucky then," Dusty said. "Would he know anything about medicine, Stevie?"

"He went to some fancy school back East to learn doctoring," the girl replied. "Or so he told me one night when he got drunk. He was thrown out of it, though. That made him wild, thinking about it. Then he'd get liquored up and lick me good."

"Most likely he knew about appendicitis, Dusty," Betty remarked. "Enough to recognize it. So he let Seth die, maybe even helped him on the way, thinking to buy the ranch."

"That was his idea," said Stevie. "Then he learned about Sandy and sent a hired gun either to kill him or to stop him from getting here in time to pay off the back taxes."

"That'd be Paco Murphy," Dusty put in.

"I think that was his name. Tony wasn't too keen on using him, wanted somebody better for the job but couldn't get anybody right then. He said Murphy was too nosy for his liking and felt sure that he'd been listening outside the office one day while he—Tony, that is—was talking to Tenby about the mine."

"He guessed right, Stevie. At least I figure Murphy knew about the mine."

Suddenly Stevie shot to her feet, winced, and sat down again. Her strained face lifted to Dusty's, and she gasped, "Hell, Ed. I just remembered. There's a place down south of here where hired guns hang out between jobs. That's where Tony got Murphy, Damon, and Ortega from. Well, he sent a man down there as soon as he heard that you'd escaped, to hire every gun there."

"Where is this place?" Dusty demanded.

"Twenty miles off at least," Becque answered, standing with Red at the open door. "That'd be the Robles place, wouldn't it, Stevie?"

"Yes. Tony wants help for when you come back, Ed."

"We'll have to take him tonight then," Dusty stated.

"Now?" said Red hopefully.

"Soon," Dusty said. "Has Towcester found the mine yet, Stevie?"

"Not that I know of," the girl replied. "He used to take me buggy riding on the Lazy M so nobody would guess what he was at. Then Tenby would go out and check any likely place for us. Tenby's a pretty fair miner if he's kept off the bottle. Say, Mrs. McGraw, that's Tony's gun you've got there."

Before leaving the Lazy M, Betty had decided that she might need a weapon and wanted something more effective than her

Remington double derringer. So she tucked the Metropolitan revolver into her waistband. Although Dusty had made a few inquiries about the ownership of the gun, he had failed until that moment to learn anything about it.

"I should have guessed," Dusty growled. "A gun like that'd be just the thing for a gambler. Only he played it clever, talking about the derringer in his jacket pocket."

"He wears a holster built into his vest," Stevie said. "And that gun's one of a pair."

"A vest holster!" Dusty exclaimed.

"Tony bought it from the man who made one for Wes Hardin," Stevie told him.

"And I saw Cousin Wes wearing his just after he bought it," Dusty replied. "Lord. I've been blind."

"Apart from Grandpappy, nobody's right all the time." Betty smiled.

"Uncle Devil's all wrong about me," Red objected.

"*I've* never noticed it," Betty replied. "And I'm not Mrs. McGraw, or Mrs. anybody, Stevie. Most of all, I'm not *his* wife."

"You reckon *you're* pleased about that?" asked Red. "When do we take Towcester, Cousin Dusty?"

"Let's give 'em a bit longer. Maybe those yahoos will go home and save us having to shoot any of them."

"I suppose that Towcester heard Mobstell and Cordova intended to bid for the ranch," Betty said to Stevie.

"Sure. And when he heard, he brought in Damon to act for him," Stevie answered, then turned back to Dusty. "Boy, you sure had Tony worried, pretending you'd found the mine."

"You told him—"

"Corlin beat me to it."

"How?" Dusty asked. "I followed him to the saloon and watched him go up to his room—"

"Which's right over Tony's office," Stevie explained. "With a trapdoor in the floor and a rope ladder ready to fasten and lower down. That's how Tony met the hired guns or anybody else he didn't want to chance being seen going in or coming out of his office."

"I suppose Towcester decided to use that Mexican killer after Corlin pretended to be looking for Cordova that first day," Dusty said. "It didn't strike me at the time, but Corlin wouldn't've been carrying the papers when he was looking for Cordova. But he thought fast when he saw me, knew Mobstell'd be in the saloon, and asked for Cordova."

"That's just how it happened," Stevie said. "He passed word for a Mexican killer to Robles. Then to make sure you kept thinking right, he dressed as a vaquero and stalked your range so that somebody would see him from a distance."

"Somebody did." Betty smiled.

"They decided to try to kill Sandy, or whoever he is, first if they could," Stevie went on. "Tony said he's such a hothead that it ought to be easy to sucker him into a fight."

"And he was right." Betty sniffed. "How about Corlin?"

"He was scared when he heard that Ed was a Texas Ranger and wanted money to run out," Stevie answered. "So Tony promised to send him some during the evening. Then he laid the trap for Ed; only it went wrong."

"Not by much," Dusty said quietly.

"I'm sorry about what happened, Ed," the girl told him contritely. "If there had been any other way— I even thought you might be tough, fast, and smart enough to get me away from Tony that first day here. Then I learned, or thought you were a Ranger captain and—"

"Sure, Stevie," Dusty interrupted. "I may still do it."

"What?"

"Get you away from him," Dusty said.

16

Standing at the bar of the Golden Goose, Towcester looked across the room to where Frenchy Becque entered. For a moment the noise of the room wavered as its occupants wondered what brought the Wells Fargo agent there at such a late hour. Before the customers could resume their activities, Becque's voice rang out.

"I've called the sheriff for you, Marshal. Figured you'd want him ready to lend a hand."

"Huh?" grunted Tenby, sitting moodily at a table, watching other men sink whiskey while he had to make do with the schooner of beer that was all Towcester allowed him to take. His fingers drummed on the shotgun beside the glass as he glanced at his employer for advice. None came, so he went on. "Yeah. That's what I wanted done."

"Got an answer, too," Becque went on loudly before the talk could well up again. "The sheriff told me to tell you who Ed Marsden is."

Towcester could almost see the ripple of interest running through the crowd and wondered how he might prevent Becque from giving the information publicly. The chance to suppress the news did not arise.

"Who is he?" Tenby muttered.

"He's Dusty Fog!"

That, while not what Towcester expected to hear, created something of a sensation among the rest of those present. The name Becque spoke passed around the room, and various unofficial deputies exchanged worried glances. Only the saloon-keeper appeared to be unaffected by what he heard.

"Fog or Marsden!" he shouted. "He still killed Corlin in cold blood."

"So everybody reckons," said Becque. "Only I'd hate like hell to be the one who tells him when he comes in with the Lazy M crew and Ole Devil's floating outfit backing his play."

"We haven't seen either Mark Counter or the Ysabel Kid in town," Towcester pointed out, watching the air of uneasy apprehension creep over his guests.

"I thought I saw them over to the Lazy M's house yesterday while I was out there hunting for a deer," Becque replied. "Want anything else doing, Marshal?"

"Naw!" grunted Tenby after a glance at Towcester.

"Reckon I'll be going then."

After Becque left, the same uneasy silence continued. Towcester glared around for a moment and then told the bartender to start livening things up. One of the unofficial deputies set down his half-filled glass and shoved back his chair. Yawning ostentatiously, he nodded to the saloonkeeper. "Thanks for the drinks, only I reckon I'd best be getting home now."

"Hey! Is that the time?" another man said, staring pointedly at the wall clock. "I'll have to be moving on."

The rest of the men who had volunteered to hunt down "Ed Marsden" found a similar need to leave the saloon. Not even Towcester's offer of another drink for the road brought a change of mind. Muttering their excuses, the unofficial deputies headed for the doors at a pace one did not normally see them use when leaving a saloon. In a very short time after Becque had delivered his message, only Towcester, Tenby, the bartender, and two bouncers remained for the girls to entertain.

Annoyance twisted Towcester's face as he watched the men go. It had been his hope that the unofficial deputies would remain all night, drinking his cheapest liquor and being kept in a state of righteous indignation against "Ed Marsden." Then, when the small Texan returned with friends to back his play, Towcester would have had help available. Already a fair amount of whiskey had passed down parched throats and many promises of what "Marsden" could expect on his arrival had been given out. Yet as soon as they learned his true identity, the unofficial deputies ran like curs with tails between their legs.

However, things were not too bad in Towcester's opinion. "Marsden," or Dusty Fog, would not reach the Lazy M until the small hours of the morning and might hold off his return until daylight. By the time he reached San Garcia, help in the form of Robles's hired guns ought to be very close.

"What now, boss?" Tenby asked, fingering his shotgun.

"We stay on here all night," Towcester replied. "Let the gals out the back and lock it up. If Mars—Fog comes, he'll have to use the front door."

While one bouncer dealt with the girls, the other locked the two side doors. On his way back to the bar, the second man glanced through the front windows. What he saw brought him to a halt.

"Boss! Becque's across the street talking to two fellers."

"Who are they?" Towcester demanded.

"One's ole Cactus from the Lazy M, and the other—hell, it's Sandy McGraw!"

"Is Fog with them?"

"Not that I can see."

Before any more could be said, the second bouncer returned hurriedly. "Somebody's at the house, boss!" he said. "The light was on in Stevie's bedroom, and I saw a gal looking out of the window."

"Stevie's there," Towcester answered.

"Only this warn't her. She ducked back fast when the gals came out, but I recognized her. It's McGraw's missus."

"McGraw nothing!" Towcester spit out. "Corlin was right. He's not McGraw."

"If Marsden's Dusty Fog, that's Red Blaze out there," the bartender said. "He's Fog's cousin—and so's that black-haired gal or I miss my guess."

"They got to Stevie!" Towcester snarled, ignoring the man.

All too well he knew how Stevie regarded him. With that thought in mind, he jerked his eyes toward the ceiling. Stevie knew the secret of the room over his office and would pass on the information to Dusty Fog when she learned that he was not a Texas Ranger. An agile man, skilled with a rope, could easily gain an entrance at the rear. Then he would—

"Get upst—" Towcester started to say.

"Becque and them other two're coming across the street, boss!" the first bouncer reported.

And the door of Towcester's office jerked open.

As the saloonkeeper feared, Dusty Fog had found little difficulty in entering the building. Using the rope Cactus had collected from the waiting horses, Dusty threw a loop over a projecting piece of the roof. Then he climbed up, gently broke a pane of glass in a window, and unfastened its catch. After pausing only long enough to draw up the carbine, Dusty moved cautiously to the room's door. All the saloon's doors had locks controlled by a master key, one of which Stevie possessed. Eager to take revenge on the man who made her life a living hell, the girl had given Dusty the means to carry out his plan.

After crossing the deserted upstairs passage, Dusty entered the room over Towcester's office. He first found the trapdoor and inched it up carefully until he was sure the office below was empty. After lowering the ladder, he went to the window and signaled to his waiting friends. Then, while Becque entered the barroom, Dusty climbed down into the office.

Dusty had counted on the power of his name and knowledge of the floating outfit's fighting prowess to scare off at least some of the unofficial deputies. From what he saw through the office window, that part of his scheme had worked even better than he had hoped. During the clatter and chatter of the men's and girls' leaving, Dusty unlocked the office door. He signaled to his friends through the window and returned to the door, ready to burst in on Towcester's remaining group.

It was a good plan, worthy of the man whose strategy during the war had caused many Yankee officers to tear their hair in impotent fury. Unfortunately for its successful conclusion, Towcester recognized the danger just a shade too soon.

Up flicked Towcester's right hand as Dusty made an appearance. It disappeared under his jacket and emerged holding the second Metropolitan revolver. At the same moment Tenby swung around, moving with surprising speed compared to his normal lethargic pace. Already walking toward it, the bartender changed to a leap for the waiting sawed-off ten-gauge. Both bouncers grabbed at their guns.

While Towcester could draw very fast, he had learned only the kind of shooting required by a professional gambler. He could deliver a hit on a man-sized target with blinding speed across the width of a poker table but lacked accuracy at any longer range. Standing some forty feet from Towcester, Dusty heard the bullet strike the wall inches to his left.

Thrusting himself forward, Dusty landed on a table. It turned over through his weight, depositing him on the floor but hiding most of him from the men at the bar. Up came the carbine, nestling into his shoulder as he sighted at Tenby and squeezed the trigger. Maybe over eight hundred yards the 26-grain powder charge of the B. Tyler Henry cartridge lacked the punch of a Sharp's buffalo rifle, but up close it delivered the 216-grain flat-nosed bullet well enough. Designed to lessen the chance of a premature explosion when jolted in the magazine tube, the bullet's shape caused it to mushroom on impact, creating shock and tissue damage out of all proportion to the comparatively weak power of the charge. Caught in the chest, Tenby slammed backward. His shotgun bellowed, but the barrels no longer pointed toward Dusty.

Swiftly Dusty flicked the carbine's lever, throwing out an empty case and feeding his next bullet into the chamber. Tenby still held the shotgun, bracing himself against the wall and trying to line it. Changing his aim slightly, Dusty sent the second bullet into the marshal's head.

Lead cut the air over Dusty's head, slapping into the table even as Tenby crumpled and slid to the floor. Twisting around, Dusty saw the first bouncer's revolver still kicked high with its recoil. Before the man could recock the gun and fire again, Dusty's carbine drove a bullet through his shoulder and tumbled him into the wall.

Feet thudded on the sidewalk, and the batwing doors burst open. Coming through them, Red Blaze whipped his Spencer carbine up and cut loose at the bartender. Caught undecided about which menace to handle, the bartender hesitated just too long. Hit between the eyes by Red's bullet, he pitched over and fell out of sight, the sawed-off shotgun clattering to the floor by his side.

On Red's heels, Cactus lunged around, and the old Colt revolving rifle let out an awesome bellow. The second bouncer threw one bullet in Dusty's direction and then went down with Cactus's solid-lead ball driven between his ribs.

Showing the same speed with which he drew his gun, Towcester turned and flung himself over the bar. Splinters sprayed up from the top of the counter as Becque fired at the saloonkeeper, but Towcester went uninjured out of sight.

"Give it up, Towcester!" Dusty called, moving around the table and lining his carbine at the bar.

"Try and make me!" the saloonkeeper yelled back, and flung himself along to grab up the bartender's discarded shotgun.

The move saved his life. Aiming at the sound of Towcester's voice, Dusty sent four bullets driving through the front of the bar in the space of two seconds. Although he spaced the shots along the bar, he did not go quite far enough to catch his man.

"Give up now, Towcester?" Dusty asked, but the man made no reply. "Cactus!"

"Yo!" came the oldster's reply.

"Get around to the back of the building and watch that cellar door Stevie told us about."

"She's done already, Cap'n," Cactus answered, and left the room.

"Watch the street and make sure nobody cuts in, Frenchy," Dusty went on.

"I'll show them my deputy sheriff's badge," Becque replied. "And if that doesn't work, I'll put my faith in Tenby's scatter-gun."

Behind the bar Towcester writhed in fury at the words, for he had planned to make his escape through the cellar after using the entrance close to him. He had also hoped that at least some of the men who had drunk his whiskey earlier would return to his aid. Neither hope could now materialize. Clearly Stevie had told Dusty Fog everything about the saloon and so blocked off the last avenue of escape. Towcester did not doubt that Becque held the office of deputy sheriff, although the other had never made the fact known, and the men who backed Tenby earlier would not go against a peace officer.

That left Towcester with only one choice: to stay put and wait out the time until Robles's men arrived. If sufficient hired guns came, they would overawe the town and rescue him.

The point had not escaped Dusty's attention. Nor did the small Texan underestimate the danger of trying to take Towcester in his present position. Remembering the bartender's shotgun, Dusty put aside any thoughts of making a concerted appearance with Red at each end of the bar. He did not doubt that Towcester now held the wicked weapon ready for use. With its cut-down barrels, the shotgun would spray out its charge in a murderous manner. Anybody facing it at that range must be caught in its pattern of death.

Of course, if Dusty and Red timed their moves correctly, one of them would be certain to get Towcester, but the other was just as sure to be killed.

While waiting for Cactus to return with his rope, Dusty had questioned Stevie and learned all he could about Towcester. One aspect of the man's nature struck Dusty while listening to the girl: Towcester's obsession and pride of ownership. Anything Towcester possessed belonged to him alone, and he protected it jealously. Once he had ordered the girl to make herself attractive to Seth McGraw and had beaten her brutally because he felt she had gone too far. Then there was his attitude to anyone who tried to damage the saloon's fittings, especially two items of them.

Remembering that, Dusty swung up his carbine and started to shoot. Firing as fast as he could work the lever, he sent bullet after bullet crashing into the chandelier. Glass shattered in a hideous jangle of sound as Towcester's prize fitting disintegrated under the hail of lead. Although Dusty could not see Towcester, he guessed the man was able to watch the destruction reflected in the bar's mirror.

Red watched Dusty and guessed what his cousin hoped to do. At the same time Red recalled that Dusty did not wear a gun belt and must have few bullets left in the carbine's twelve-shot magazine. Dropping to one knee, Red drew his left-side Colt and sent it sliding across the floor in his cousin's direction.

"Dusty!" he called, and swung the Spencer to his shoulder.

Counting his shots automatically, Dusty knew that the carbine held only two more bullets. Yet Towcester still did not make an appearance. So Dusty changed his aim and fired twice at the bar mirror.

Snarling in fury, Towcester burst into sight at the end of the bar. Dusty dropped the empty carbine and dived toward Red's revolver. Going over in a roll, he caught up the gun and landed on his back. Towcester's shotgun boomed, its lead slashing the air. Something hot knifed into Dusty's leg, and he started to fan the Colt's hammer. Three times he shot. Twice splinters flew from the bar, moving closer to Towcester. On the third shot the saloonkeeper jerked, and the muzzle of his shotgun turned just far enough for its charge to miss Dusty as Towcester pressed the trigger. Mingled with the roar of the shotgun, Red's Spencer barked. The top of Towcester's head seemed to burst open and a grayish pulp sprayed into the air. Then he collapsed to the sawdust-spotted floor.

"Did he get you, Dusty?" Red asked, running to his cousin's side.

"One ball did, in the leg," Dusty replied. "Make sure he's finished."

"If he's not," Red said dryly, looking at the hideous mess of Towcester's head, "he's the toughest cuss I've ever seen."

17

While Dr. Paczek dug a .32-caliber buckshot ball from Dusty's leg, Becque cleared him of the false accusation. Most people in town accepted the evidence of the two clean Colts produced from the Wells Fargo safe. Any lingering doubts departed on hearing that Paczek had extracted a Winchester bullet from Corlin's body and that Becque had found in Towcester's office a rifle that had been fired.

A deputation of well-armed citizens greeted Robles's hired guns at the edge of San Garcia and made it plain that their presence in town would be neither needed nor tolerated. Seeing the determined faces of the citizens and realizing there would be no payment for fighting, the gunhands turned their horses to ride back the way they came.

Two days later Sandy and Sarah McGraw arrived at their new home. After they had settled in, Dusty told them everything he knew.

"I don't reckon you'll have any more trouble, Sandy," he

finished, rubbing the injured leg. "We settled the man behind it all."

"Did he kill Uncle Seth?" Sandy demanded.

"That's one thing we'll never know for sure," Dusty said. "Maybe he did, or perhaps that illness saved him the trouble."

"He would have tried sooner or later," Betty added.

"How about that girl Stevie?" Sarah asked.

"She's selling the Golden Goose and going to Kansas," Dusty replied. "It's only right, and she'll keep quiet about what Towcester was after. None of his hired help other than Tenby and Murphy knew about the mine, and they can't talk. Nor will Cactus, Frenchy Becque, or any of us."

"What do you aim to do about it, Sandy?" Red inquired. "We searched Towcester's place and never found a hint about where the mine might be."

For a moment Sandy did not reply, thinking of the range through which he rode to reach the ranch house.

"I saw a silver strike once," he said quietly. "Folks flocked in, tearing up the range, ruining it. And all the thieves, macs, lobby lizzies, and scum came swarming in like buzzards to a dead cow. Lordy lord. I'd sure hate to turn that loose up here."

"So?" Dusty asked.

"So as far as I'm concerned, ole Jim Bowie's lost mine can stay lost. Uncle Seth willed me this place as a ranch, not a mining camp."

Thinking back to what he had also seen in areas following the discovery of precious metals, Dusty felt Sandy made the right decision. The small man looked at his cousins and read that they agreed. So Dusty rose to his feet. McGraw's inheritance was safe. No longer did Sandy and Sarah need fear the unknown menace that had threatened their lives. With his work in San Garcia done, Dusty wanted to start out and return to the OD Connected.